PARANORMAL COZY MYSTERY

Charms & Firearms

TRIXIE SILVERTALE

Sittin' On A Goldmine Productions, L.L.C.

info@sittinonagoldmine.co

www.sittinonagoldmine.co

ISBN: 978-1-7340221-7-9

Trixie Silvertale
Charms and Firearms: Paranormal Cozy Mystery : a novel / by Trixie Silvertale — 1st ed.

[1. Paranormal Cozy Mystery — Fiction. 2. Cozy Mystery — Fiction. 3. Amateur Sleuths — Fiction. 4. Female Sleuth — Fiction. 5. Wit and Humor — Fiction.] 1. Title.

CHAPTER 1

No matter how many times I press the embossed plaster medallion that opens the secret bookcase-door from my swanky apartment to the Rare Books Loft, it still blows me away! My grandmother left this entire bookshop to me. I mumble under my breath, "You've come a long way, baby."

A year ago, I lived in a rundown studio apartment in Sedona, Arizona. If you had suggested that a frumpy little man, with a large mustache and a wrinkled brown suit, would knock on my door and hand me an envelope filled with a new future . . . I would've laughed in your face, and likely refused to make your coffee order on the grounds that you were insane.

At the time, I was a broke barista with sporadic hot water, but today I'm "runway walking" across a fine Persian rug in a pair of T-strap Valentino's while the sound of a vintage Marchesa swishes over my ample thighs.

I'm hosting a fundraiser for the Pin Cherry Harbor animal shelter. I've never hosted a fundraiser before—not because I don't have a soft spot in my heart for a number of charitable causes, but because I've never had money.

So, today I'm hosting for two reasons: (1) my dad's new girlfriend is on the board of directors at the animal shelter; and (2) my grandmother, God rest her, absolutely loves to dress me up like a little doll. And you heard me correctly. My grandmother passed away and left the wealth of her five ex-husbands and the beautiful Bell, Book & Candle to me. However, her ghost still resides in the bookshop, and I also received her spoiled-rotten cat as part of the bargain.

"Now don't you go saying anything bad about Mr. Cuddlekins. That cat has saved your life more times than I care to mention."

And yet she's mentioning it. I spin on my five-inch designer heels and firmly fix a fist on each of my hips. "Grams, I can't believe we're having this discussion again. If these lips aren't moving, you're not part of the conversation. No thought-dropping. And definitely no interjecting your opinion into my internal dialogue."

"It wasn't for my sake, dear. I was defending Pyewacket."

"Re-ow."

And that would be Mr. Cuddlekins, who's known as Pyewacket to the rest of us. He's an eerily intuitive fur baby with an addiction to children's sugared cereal and a penchant for getting his whiskers into death-defying trouble.

"Hey, are you gonna come down here and help me set up? Or am I gonna need to hire more servants, Your Highness?" The cacophonous intonations of my volunteer employee, Twiggy, drift up from the first floor.

She was my grandmother's best friend in life, and her severe grey pixie, dungarees, and biker boots stomp around my bookshop free of charge. She works for the entertainment, not the cash.

With a pleasing inhalation of book-rich air, I firmly grip the wrought-iron railing on the circular staircase leading down to the main floor of the bookshop and do my best to navigate the narrow wedge-shaped treads as I descend into the bowels of the store. I unhook the "No Admittance" chain at the bottom of the stairs, but before I can even step off the final stair I'm already being admonished.

Twiggy's disembodied voice echoes off the tin-plated ceiling. "You be sure to hook the chain back up, doll. This place is going to be crawling with looky-loos."

"Unless I missed a memo, the silent auction is set up in the Rare Books Loft. I think we're going to have to allow people access if we want them to actually place bids." I grin at my own witty response.

Twiggy stomps out from between the stacks and fixes me with an irritated glare. "I wasn't born yesterday. I hired security for the event. Once they get here, I'll unhook the chain."

I roll my eyes, but don't have the guts to argue. One of the things I clearly don't grasp about my rare books collection is the actual monetary value of those ancient leather-bound tomes. The fact that the key to binding my gramma's spirit to this place was uncovered in one of them should give me a hint. I mean, it's hard to place a value on family.

Walking toward the caterer, I hope to have a more pleasant interaction. "Do you need any help setting up, Anne?"

The owner of Bless Choux, the patisserie on Third Avenue, shakes her head. "Absolutely not. I wouldn't dream of taking a chance on you getting something on that gorgeous gown."

"At least give me the delicious details, so I can plan my attack."

She beams with pride. "We have strawberry

tartlets with hazelnut chocolate paw prints, grilled eggplant canapés with smoked gouda, individually packaged souvenir sugar cookies with the shelter's logo in royal icing, and, of course, pin cherry cheesecake bars."

"My mouth is definitely watering. Everything looks amazing. Are you sure there's nothing I can do?"

She blushes and feigns a curtsy. "Thank you. I've got things under control here. Maybe Amaryllis could use a hand at the sign-in table?"

I glance toward a small table set up in front of the colorful children's book section and catch my father, Jacob Duncan, proudly appraising my outfit. "Hey, Dad."

"Your grandmother must be—would be so proud." He gives me a wink and his cheeks flush a little at the slip up. He and I share our genetically bone-white blonde hair and our mysterious grey eyes. And we also share the secret of the ghost of grandmothers past. Actually, my father, Twiggy, myself, and my grandmother's former lawyer Silas Willoughby are the only people who know Grams didn't actually cross over.

"Hey, Amaryllis, is there anything I can do to help?"

She looks up from a table arranged with brochures, pens, a "will call" list, and a cashbox.

The little wrinkles around her brown eyes are the only indication of worry.

I haven't known her long, but she's a competent attorney that worked for my grandfather, before he passed, and continues to manage the Duncan estate that was handed down to my father.

"Oh, Mitzy, I honestly think I have everything covered here. But I would really appreciate it if you'd greet the guests and let them know about the silent auction items upstairs."

Of all the possible tasks she could give me, social butterfly would be my last choice. "Of course, happy to help." I hope that was more convincing out loud than it sounded in my head.

My dad crosses the room in a few large strides and scoops one strong arm around my shoulders. He leans his six-foot-and-change frame toward me and whispers in my ear. "At the risk of sounding too proud, Mom did a real nice job with the outfit. She always was partial to Marchesa."

He gives me a little squeeze and my heart warms with the comfort of family that was stolen from me when my mother died in a car-versus-commuter-train accident ten years ago. At that time I had no idea who my father was, and with no other relatives to care for me, I wound up in the foster system. After more than six years of hard knocks under my belt, I learned to take care of myself and bury my emotions under a thick outer shell. When I quit my barista job at Hot Kafka in Arizona and took a very smelly bus to almost-Canada, I had no idea my strange, triangular brass key would open a bookshop and a treasure trove of family secrets.

My Ghost-ma, as I lovingly call her, passed away at sixty-one after more than a year of severe illness. However, thanks to her attorney/alchemist, Silas, she was able to stay on this side of the veil, complete with her many lovely rings, multiple strands of pearls and a burgundy silk-and-tulle—you guessed it—Marchesa gown. She was also fortunate enough to be able to take on the ghost-age of her choice, which for her is thirty-five. So even though she's my grams, her appearance makes her feel almost like an older sister.

"Awww, Mitzy, that's the sweetest thing." Grams blasts into 3-D right before my eyes, like an old-fashioned camera flash bulb.

And I nearly pee from the shock. Since I'm surrounded by strangers and can't give Grams a proper lecture, I'm forced to send her a telepathic scolding. *Grams, I know you get a real kick out of scaring the bejeezus out of me, but I'm all dressed up and I'm short on adult diapers. So, if you could keep the pop-ins to a minimum and use the slow, sparkly reentry that we've agreed on, I would greatly appreciate it.*

"Of course, dear, how silly of me."

If you assumed her tone was more patronizing than apologetic, you'd be quite accurate. Maybe you're a budding psychic like me.

The food is laid out with flair on the buffet table, and the hors d'oeuvres and pastries look and smell delicious. Despite my recovering alcoholic grandmother's protests, we will be serving champagne. Both Amaryllis and I agree that bidding tends to increase with the application of a little "social lubricant."

Before I have a chance to get into another debate with Grams, the door to the alleyway opens and two barking dogs tear into the bookshop

I have no idea where Pyewacket is hiding, but those dogs are in for a terrible surprise if they think they can outsmart a spoiled caracal! "Twiggy, where in all of Narnia did they come from?"

She fixes me with an exasperated stare, or perhaps I should refer to it as her usual expression. "We can't very well raise money for an animal shelter without showing some animals. That finicky feline of your grandmother's sure as shellac ain't gonna let nobody pet him."

"Well, you'd better get those dogs under control before Pye catches their scent. They'll never make it out of here alive."

"As you wish, Your Highness."

Twiggy shuts the dogs in the back room, and I

hope, for their sakes, Pyewacket isn't already hiding in there.

The first guest to arrive is our local veterinarian Ledo Sikanen. Pushing his wheelchair is my favorite waitress, Tally. Her hair is scooped into its signature tight, flame-red bun sitting atop her head, and she is bedecked in a lovely blue skirt and sweater set.

"Doc Ledo, so good to see you. How are the modifications going at the clinic? Were you able to get the new adjustable surgical table?"

Doc Ledo shakes my hand warmly as he replies. "Things couldn't be better. It took me a month or so to adjust to the wheelchair, and right now, I'm only working three days a week in the clinic. But I'm assisting the traveling vet on surgeries and, if all goes well, I should be back to work full-time next month and handling all the surgeries myself."

Tally smiles and lovingly pats her brother on the shoulder. "You know him, always the optimist. Some days he acts like that hit-and-run accident was the best thing that ever happened to him." She shrugs her shoulders and casts her emotion-filled eyes heavenward.

"Well, I'm glad things are working out, and I know your patients will be pleased to have you back full-time. Not that the traveling veterinarian isn't a lovely woman, but when I had to take Pyewacket in for his rabies shot last month, she almost lost a finger."

Doc Ledo and I share a chuckle, and the flick of a stubby tail catches my eye. I point to the top of one of the bookshelves, and Ledo follows the gesture.

He grins and nods. "Oh, Pyewacket. I hear you miss me?"

Pyewacket gracefully leaps down from the bookcase in a blur of tan, struts across the floor like he owns the place—and, let's be honest, he might as well—and rubs against the doctor's legs.

Tally and I share an uneasy glance.

Doc Ledo doesn't miss a beat. He leans down and scratches Pyewacket's head right between his black tufted ears. "I'm afraid these old legs can't fully appreciate your generous affections, Pye. But I sure am happy to see you looking so healthy. If I didn't know better I'd say you never age."

"Re-ow." Can confirm.

I chuckle under my breath. I've often thought the same thing about Pyewacket and always wondered how old he really is. Grams claims she won him in an "off the books" Scrabble game, but I seem to remember my dad sharing memories of Pyewacket being around when he was a child.

No time for that conundrum. "I hope you'll both excuse me. Guests are pouring in and it's my job as the hostess with the most-ess to get them properly orientated and make sure they know about the silent auction items upstairs." As soon as I say it, I feel sick to my stomach.

Tally's eyes widen.

"I'm sorry, Doc. That was really thoughtless."

Doc Ledo reaches out and grabs my hand. He gives it a fatherly pat. "No need to apologize, Mitzy. I know your heart's in the right place, and hosting this event is a huge undertaking. I'm sure I can convince Tally to run upstairs and place a few bids for me."

I smile uncomfortably and can't seem to get my feet to move.

Tally nods. "Well, you'd better get to the rest of the guests."

As I shuffle off, I feel the heat rising in my cheeks. Hurrying toward the steady stream of potential donors, a fresh wave of warm swirls through my tummy when I see a familiar and handsome face. "Mr. Bombay, how good of you to come to our little soirée."

Rory scoops an arm around my waist and leans his face dangerously close to mine. "I wouldn't miss it for the world, Mizithra."

"Well played." We both chuckle, and I'm the first to relent and abandon formalities. "It's good to see you, Rory. Do you have any exciting new artifacts at the antiquities shop?"

"Perhaps I can convince you to join me in Grand Falls for lunch later this week?"

"Perhaps."

His devilish chuckle sends a ripple of tingles through my tummy, and I'm just about to abandon my hostess duties when I catch my father's stern gaze through the crowd. "Rory, we'll catch up later. I have to greet the guests."

"Of course, Mitzy. I can entertain myself."

The hairs on the back of my neck stand on end and the magic mood ring on my left hand sparks with heat. I resist the urge to look at it and see if there's a psychic message. Instead, I swish away in my designer dress and head to the front door.

Odell must have closed the diner early. His grey buzz cut bobs up and down as he jostles through the line winding along the red velvet ropes, and the sight of him brings a genuine smile to my face.

I shake several hands, distribute a few brochures, and highlight a couple of our amazing silent auction items as I work my way through the new arrivals.

When I finally reach Odell, he's looking crankier than usual. "Thanks for braving the crowds."

He shrugs and exhales. "Isadora always had a soft spot for animals."

"Grams would be touched that you came." I give him the canned "welcome" speech and add that I promise to see him for breakfast in the morning.

Twiggy still hasn't unhooked the chain. If we want to get these silent auction items out the door, I'll have to start the bidding. Walking toward the circular staircase, the sound of the metal door to the alley slamming shut catches my attention. I look toward the makeshift stage under the large six-by-six windows at the front of the bookstore and Twiggy is fussing over the two pups on display.

Definitely wasn't her.

A wave of concern washes over me and I hurry toward the back door, running smack dab into the delicious specimen known as Sheriff Erick Harper. "Erick, I didn't expect to see you tonight."

"It's Sheriff Harper, Miss Moon. And I'm on duty. Twiggy asked me to—"

"Work security in the Rare Books Loft?" I can't help but chuckle.

He manages to keep a serious face as he nods. "10-4."

I laugh and place a hand on his arm. "Then it's your job to officially unhook the chain." I gesture toward the circular staircase.

He nods affirmatively, and a lovely strand of his blond hair falls across his face. He quickly slicks it back in place with one hand as his blue-grey eyes sparkle with playfulness. He unhooks the chain and climbs the staircase.

I can't help but watch. I mean, everybody's got a weakness. Unfortunately, my weakness tends to involve forgetting that I'm in a room full of people. And the next thing I know, I've been caught red-handed.

"Are you certain there's nothing I should know about you and the sheriff?" Rory's green eyes stare at me intently as he narrows his gaze.

My clairsentience picks up on a strong dose of jealousy, which I promptly ignore. "I don't think so. But just to be clear, I am a free agent." I give him a wink and walk toward the front of the bookstore with a little extra swish in my swagger.

CHAPTER 2

Believe it or not, I stayed up until nearly midnight going through each of the silent auction bidding sheets with Amaryllis. And in case you're not familiar with local customs, anything that lasts beyond 9:00 p.m., especially on a Thursday night, is considered patently insane. At least Grams and Pyewacket have the decency to allow me to sleep late.

In my previous life, slinging macchiatos and keeping friendships shallow, I would never have considered getting out of bed before 10:00 a.m., but now it seems indulgent to lie under my luscious, down comforter while the crisp light of midmorning leaks around the edges of my new window shades.

I find myself more and more often saying, "when in Rome." And in "Rome" folks are up at the crack of dawn, busy getting after life. I roll myself out of bed and immediately head over to turn on the space heater in the bathroom. I keep hearing the term "spring" bandied about, but my previous experience with spring in the Southwest involves beating on a poorly functioning window air conditioner and wondering if I could get away with a sleeveless shirt at work.

Up north spring unfolds a bit differently. I'm still wearing adult onesie pajamas to bed, and bundling up in a down coat and something called a stocking hat every time I leave the bookshop. I've learned a technique called layering, and today my first layer will be a lovely T-shirt bearing the phrase, "Death Before Decaf." I swipe on a little hydrating lip tint, shrug at my reflection in the antique vanity mirror and turn just in time to observe a swirling ball of sparkling light drifting toward me. "I see you, Grams."

She unfolds into her well-dressed, full-size self and takes an undeserved bow. "Aren't you proud of Pyewacket and me? We've been amusing ourselves for hours in the bookshop and didn't even disturb you."

I chuckle as a thought pops into my head. "Did you feed him?"

Grams crosses her bejeweled arms over her ample bosom and smiles a little too smugly. "I have to say, I'm getting very good at moving things. I managed to pour most of the Fruity Puffs into his bowl, and I absolutely guarantee he can hear me now."

Of course, the only thing that rattles around in my head is that ridiculous cell phone commercial, "Can you hear me now?"

Grams chuckles. "Oh, I remember that one."

"Of course you would. Sometimes I lose track of how recently you crossed over."

"Technically, dear, I didn't cross over."

"True enough."

Grams swirls around me as I walk toward the secret door. "Are you headed over to the diner?"

I stop and smile at the jealousy flickering across her spectral face. "Yes, Myrtle Isadora Johnson Linder Duncan Willamette Rogers, I'm off to Myrtle's Diner to enjoy your first husband's incredible skill behind the grill. I'll be sure to reference your charming generosity in his presence."

"Oh, Mitzy, you're such a hoot. You know, I'll always regret divorcing Odell. But he's better off without me."

I glance up at my grandmother and smile. "Grams, you and I both know he never got over you. If the fact that he never remarried isn't proof enough, I think the fact that he was by your side every day for the last year and a half of your life should prove his affection beyond a shadow of a doubt."

Shimmering tears spring from my grandmother's eyes.

"Sooner or later Silas and I are bound to figure out a way to get you an afterlife handkerchief!"

Grams laughs through her tears and slips through the wall, while I wait for the secret bookcase door to slide open.

The hairs in the back of my neck tingle as the door slides closed, and I turn to watch the candle mechanism that serves as the handle on the side of the door click back into place. But what catches my attention is the empty space on the bookshelf next to it.

"Grams!"

She pops up beside me. "What is it? What's wrong, dear?"

"Look." I point to the empty space on the shelf

"Oh no! *Saducismus Triumphatus* is missing!" She covers her open mouth with a ring-ensconced hand.

"You don't think Silas was right about Rory, do you? If he wanted to see the book, he would just ask me, right?"

Grams clutches her pearls. "You'd better call Silas at once."

As I wind down the circular staircase and out

the side door into the alley, I call my lawyer and mentor. “You’re not going to— Of course. No, you’re right. Yes . . . I understand. Let me try again. Good morning, Mr. Willoughby. We missed you at the fundraising event last night. I hope you are well.” Geez Louise this guy and his manners. I’m having a potentially devastating crisis, and he wants to waste time on niceties.

I attempt to reassert my need. “It really is urgent.”

He doesn’t bite.

“I understand. Can you just meet me at the diner? Why not? Oh, I see. I’m sure you *do* have other responsibilities besides me. But *Saducismus Triumphatus* is missing!”

His utter calm is beyond irritating.

“Right. Of course. I’ll see you then.” How am I supposed to know he’s out of town? It’s not like I manage his calendar. Anyway, he returns to Pin Cherry today and he promised to stop by the bookshop.

For now, I’m just going to focus on eating the most delicious breakfast in town and catching up on local gossip with Tally. I might even entertain my quaint new pastime of reading the newspaper. Despite the promise of spring, the frosty wind blowing across the great lake currently thawing to life in the harbor provides more than enough encouragement for me to switch from walking to a brisk jog. I push open the door to Myrtle's Diner and let the warmth embrace me.

Odell's wrinkled grin pops into the red-Formica-trimmed orders-up window and he salutes me with his spatula.

I nod.

Two regulars occupy the booth in the back corner, and a man I vaguely recognize occupies one of the four-tops by the front window. I opt for a stool at the counter, and, before I can even sit down, Tally places a steaming cup of coffee in front of me. "Thank you, Tally."

She nods, and the pencil poked through her bright-red bun bobs up and down.

The smells of fried eggs and sizzling bacon waft out of the kitchen and coax a loud growl from my stomach. I chuckle and grab the newspaper, but before I can read a single word, Odell cranks up a conversation.

"How'd the fundraiser go?"

"Great. Amaryllis had things running like a top, and she managed to get some really great items for the silent auction."

"Like what?"

"All kinds of stuff, but the one I really wanted was a weekend getaway to the Fox Mountain Ski Resort. Not that I know anything about skiing, but my dad said it's a beautiful resort and, if I was lucky, I might even catch some of the early spring flowers blooming."

Odell chuckles as a spatula scrapes across the grill. "Sounds a little tame for your taste." He enjoys additional laughter at my expense.

I take a careful sip of my wake-up juice before I reply. "I'll have you know, I'm learning to enjoy the outdoors. And I would've been only too happy to explore Fox Mountain if I hadn't been outbid by—"

"Mizithra, I was hoping to bump into you."

Unless my ears deceive me, that is the voice of the winning bidder and number one suspect in the disappearance of *Saducismus Triumphatus*. Time for one of my legendary Oscar-winning performances. I rotate slowly on my stool as I say, "Mr. Bombay."

Rory's green eyes sparkle with mischief as he bows elegantly. "At your service, Miss Moon."

"What have I told you about calling me Miss Moon?"

Rory chuckles as he takes a seat next to me at the counter. "I suppose I just keep hoping you'll punish me."

Oh dear, this fish might be too big for me to land. At this point it feels like the most prudent option is to ignore his innuendo and launch a counterattack. "So, you thought you could outbid me on the

Fox Mountain getaway and *get away* scot-free? False."

A sly grin creeps across his face as he ignores the steaming mug of java Tally places directly between us, and he continues to lean enticingly close. "I was hoping you'd say that, Mitzy."

The exotic scent of his well-traveled skin threatens to send me into a swoon of sandalwood and cardamom. I take a shallow breath and soldier on with my failing charge. "Let me guess, you got me the getaway as a present?" As soon as the words escape my lips, the be-spelled ring on my left hand burns out a fiery warning. I risk a downward glance and see the rapidly fading image of a fox. Since most of my psychic messages are vague and open to interpretation, I'm not one hundred percent sure if the message is a warning about the slyness of the fox, a reference to Fox Mountain, or simply confirmation that Rory Bombay is a hot property.

Rory's green eyes widen, but they seem to be filled with more suspicion than surprise. "What an odd thing to say. In fact, I'd like to invite you to be my 'plus one' on *my* Fox Mountain Ski Resort getaway weekend. Would you consider allowing me the privilege of teaching you to cross-country ski?"

I hesitate before uttering a reply for a couple of reasons. First of all, I don't know the first thing about skiing, and I have no idea what constitutes cross-country skiing. However, my second concern will be handled first. "If I agree, and that is a big *if*, I'll pay for my own room."

Tally slides my mouthwatering plate of scrambled eggs, chorizo, and gorgeous browned home fries onto the counter and nods supportively.

The shock that now fills Rory's eyes is one hundred percent manufactured. "Miss Moon, I'm astonished that you would assume otherwise. As my guest, you can be assured that I will cover the cost of your separate-but-equal accommodations."

I'd like to say I'm pleased with his answer, but it honestly feels a little more condescending than necessary. Maybe he heard some rumors about my wild days in Arizona and assumed I hadn't changed. For the record, I may or may not have changed. But this getaway is purely for the purposes of fact-finding, and I don't want to be distracted by letting a fox into the hen house. I'm not sure if that analogy works, but I'm pleased that I worked fox back into the mix.

"Is that smirk part of your answer?"

Oops. Once again I've gotten lost in my mind-movies and forgotten I have an audience. "I never make decisions on an empty stomach. You'll have to excuse me while I enjoy this wonderful breakfast."

Tally sets a warm cinnamon roll in front of

Rory and lays a place setting wrapped in a thin paper napkin on his left.

He looks up and hits her with his mesmerizing, woman-disarming smile, looks down at the veritable feast, and nods appreciatively. "Thank you, kind lady. This is, of course, exactly what I wanted."

Apparently, Odell's culinary mind-reading skills are catching.

I dig into my hearty breakfast and smile internally as Tally expertly refills my coffee cup, a second before I ask. I don't exactly miss being a barista, but I certainly have a first-hand appreciation for skilled, nonintrusive service. As I savor my second cup of black gold, I entertain Rory's offer. I know Grams disliked him, then she adored him after he gave me an emerald ring and a fancy dinner, but if she suspects him, as I do, of the theft of *Saducismus Triumphatus*, I'm sure she's back to serious dislike. Also, my dad's never been a fan. And Silas is mostly suspicious of anyone who shows an unnatural interest in my occult manuscripts. However, if Mr. Bombay is the thief, what better way to uncover his true intentions than to give myself an entire weekend of uninterrupted psychic messages?

Keep your friends close and your enemies closer. I'm not entirely sure which category Rory belongs in, but I want to believe he's a friend. On the off chance that he has something to do with the missing tome, this getaway weekend is just what the alchemist ordered.

"You seem to be weighing a heavy burden as you consider my offer. Should I be concerned?"

"Not at all. I accept your invitation to Fox Mountain. I insist on paying for my own room, but I'll go."

He laughs a little too eagerly as he takes my left hand. "I look forward to it. May I pick you up at the bookshop at noon?"

Wait! Is today Friday? The suddenness of the actual weekend away looms over me, and I fear I could lose my nerve. Courage, D'Artagnan. "Noon will be divine." And there I go, slipping into the unnecessary use of the word "divine" when tensions mount. I leave some cash on the counter for a tip, as is the custom in the town that tech forgot, and wave to Odell as I leave.

CHAPTER 3

Hurrying back to the bookshop, the little wheels in my mind begin to whir like the toys in *Mr. Magorium's Wonder Emporium*. What have I gotten myself into? What if Rory is responsible for the missing volume? What better place for him to get rid of me than the deserted skiing trails of a remote mountain chalet.

I grab the handle of the ornately carved wooden door at the front of the bookshop and nearly dislocate my arm with the discovery that it's locked. A distant champagne-clouded memory drifts to the surface. Right! I told Twiggy to take the morning off after our late night straightening up in the wake of the successful fundraiser. I fish out the chain under my T-shirt and retrieve the key to the Bell, Book & Candle. A weighty brass object with a triangle-shaped barrel that must be turned three times to complete the door-opening process. I insert the key and, as I turn it, my eyes fall on the carving. It's such a beautiful scene—magical wood nymphs, a centaur, a winged-horse flying in front of a full moon, and there, at the edge of the circle of frivolity, a fiendish feline who bears a striking resemblance to Pye. As I complete the third revolution of the key, the door is suddenly pushed open from the inside and knocks me on my hind end, directly onto the fortuitously positioned red-velvet ropes piled up from last night's queue.

Twiggy's cackle fills the entryway. "I've got to say, that just never gets old."

And this would be the entertainment with which I pay the dear woman.

"And I have to say, it's already ancient, decaying, and due to be burned on a pyre." My protest is met with further cackling and the door swinging shut. It would appear that Twiggy chose to come in before noon, despite the instructions of her boss.

As soon as I enter, Grams bursts through the ceiling and insists I share every detail of my breakfast. Luckily, I was expecting this ghostly assault, which prevented any additional pants accidents.

"How was the coffee?"

"The coffee was delicious, as always. And just in case you were wondering, I had my usual breakfast and I enjoyed it just as much as usual. No more, no less."

Eager to show off her expanding powers affecting physical objects, Grams grabs the top of my stocking hat and pulls it off. Then promptly drops it on the ground as she claps her ethereal hands in celebration.

I stoop to retrieve the hat as Grams' voice hits a lower octave. "And what did he want?"

"He? He who?"

My innocent gaze is met with a well-manicured ghost fist on each of her hips. "Don't get cute with me. That Rory Bombay was banging around the front door less than an hour ago. I think it's safe to assume he headed straight to the diner after getting no answer here."

"Oh, Rory stopped by the diner and had a cup of coffee and a cinnamon roll. Anything else?"

"I may look thirty-five, dear, but keep in mind, I have nearly twice that much experience reading body language—not to mention my on-again/off-again clairvoyance. I'd say there's a little more to the story. Dish."

She's definitely got me backed into a corner. Even if I don't reveal what we talked about out loud, she knows full well I'll be thinking about it in ten seconds flat. I may as well tell the story on my own terms.

"I think that is best, dear."

As it turns out, Grams is surprisingly supportive of my espionage plans. She agrees that Rory definitely tops the suspect list, and she believes that subterfuge is our best plan. Since our strategy is to put Rory at ease and allow me to get some baseline psychic readings, we pack accordingly.

Grams insists that I ditch my snarky T-shirts in exchange for curve hugging sweaters and even a delicious royal-blue sweater *dress*. She assures me that the Top of the Lift is a fine dining establishment not to be missed.

I hate the idea of being overdressed, but I realize Rory is a sophisticated man who'll certainly have precisely the right wardrobe for every event scheduled over the course of our getaway.

However, I put my foot down when Grams attempts to convince me that some sort of winter knee-breeches and something called gaiters are required for cross-country skiing.

"That is *A Bridge Too Far*, Grams. I'm not crossing it, because I have absolutely no interest in experiencing anything that happens on the other side of a bridge that requires me to wear breeches."

"I can assure you that you'll regret that decision after an hour on the trail."

Regardless of whatever ghost snit she's throwing, I grab a cute pair of regular-length purple ski pants, a fake-fur-trimmed ski jacket, several pairs of wool socks, two pairs of mittens, a scarf, and something called a balaclava. I don't think I'll wear the balaclava, but as a film school dropout, I'd be remiss in leaving such an iconic piece of winter wardrobe behind.

Before I can really enjoy a good chuckle about how I'd look like a true, big-screen bank robber wearing that mask, I remember my family reality isn't all that far from my whimsical fantasy.

Grams swirls in close and says, "It's not your fault, dear. You didn't even know him then." She drifts aimlessly toward the ceiling, like a feather on the wind, and I drop onto the padded mahogany bench in my amazing, right out of *Sex and the City* meets *Confessions of a Shopaholic*, closet.

In case I forgot to mention it earlier, nearly sixteen or seventeen years ago my father was involved in one of the largest armed robberies ever to take place up north. He served fifteen years in the state penitentiary and, honestly, came out a changed man. He managed to shed the layers of entitlement that wealth and privilege had padded around him, and he's doing everything he can to make amends to society. In fact, he's in the final stages of prepping the land next door for the construction of the Duncan Restorative Justice Foundation. My dad, Jacob Duncan, plans to offer assistance to ex-convicts in need of employment, as well as legal funding and representation for wrongly convicted prisoners.

When I first learned that my father had purchased the building right next door to me, I worried a tiny bit about being smothered. But once construction was put on hold due to an inferno, which destroyed the original landmark structure, he and I had a wonderful conversation about his vision for the foundation and his hopes for building a relationship with me. Boundaries were set and approved.

So, while he's selling his family's enormous mansion located at the end of a gorgeous private drive on the shores of the region's great lake, I'm looking forward to him living in his penthouse apartment next door. We even jokingly discussed putting in an enclosed walkway across the third floor, joining our respective buildings in a Frida Kahlo/Diego Rivera homage.

He was more excited about that than me. Although, I have managed to get myself in plenty of trouble since arriving in town, and I suppose it's natural for a father to want to look out for his little girl—even if she is nearly twenty-two.

Grams floats back down and fervently nods her agreement. "He really does want to make up for lost time, Mitzy. I know he's grateful that you're giving him the chance." She places her phantom hand on my back and I feel the strange sensation, to which I'm becoming accustomed: warm energy with little or no weight, but a great deal of comfort.

"Thanks. I appreciate your support in my decision to take things slow."

Grams arches one perfectly drawn brow, crosses her arms, and fixes me with a stare tinged with judgment. "Speaking of taking things slow, I do hope you packed your reindeer onesie pajamas!" She manages to hold the stern look for a split second before she collapses into ghostly guffaws.

My retort melts in my chest as I bask in the warmth of family. But she's not wrong. No negligées grace this suitcase. I'm on a fact-finding mission to infiltrate the enemy, and I plan on giving nothing away.

Grams swipes at a sparkly tear in the corner of her eye. "That's my girl."

I roll my eyes at the double entendre and throw an extra phone charger in my suitcase, unable to remember if I packed one. As I zip it closed, I wonder if I'm ready for a weekend getaway.

"No time for second thoughts! He's here!"

I point meaningfully to my lips and shake my head. "Grams, if these aren't moving—"

She waves away my protest with a swipe of her hand. "Be careful, and check in every day." She points to a stack of 3 x 5 cards and a pen. "Silas should be back later today, and I'll get him up to speed with my notecards."

I nod. I keep forgetting that I'm the only one that can hear Grams. Silas has a set of spectacles he worked some alchemical juju on so that he can see her, but he still hasn't devised a way to hear her. However, it actually seems that Pye might be joining the ranks of those who can potentially see and hear her, but since he speaks his own complex, yet non-English, language, he's not always the best ally.

The three gongs of the doorbell echo through the bookshop and signify a visitor at the alley entrance. I take a deep breath and roll my suitcase out of the apartment.

My tummy feels quite tingly and my heart races as I wonder what treasures await on Fox Mountain.

CHAPTER 4

THE DRIVE to the ski resort takes us along the picturesque banks of the great lake nestled in Pin Cherry Harbor. The melting ice floes provide a constantly changing tableau. A mosaic of pack ice floats amongst grey-black waves far out on the horizon, while on the shore massive frozen crests of water glisten in the pale spring sun. The size of some of these icy ramparts is breathtaking, and I find it impossible to believe that they'll all be melted away in less than a couple months.

"A present for your thoughts?"

My eyes lazily drift toward my traveling companion, and I realize I have no idea how much time has passed. I smile absently as I glance at the object in Rory's hand.

A gorgeous gold leather box. A single red ribbon.

"A present! For me?"

He smiles mischievously and winks. "I don't see anyone else in the car."

I grab the present before he can change his mind. It's hard to adequately describe how exciting it is to get a gift, after so many birthdays without a family. I sincerely hope it's not a pair of socks. For those of you who don't know, presents are few and far between in the foster system and they are always something useful—something that you must have—not something extravagant that you'd spent all your sleepless nights wishing for . . .

I slip off the ribbon and open the fancy box. The hinges creak a little, but my gasp covers the sound. As I'm about to reach in, the scene from *Pretty Woman* flashes through my mind and I cast a suspicious glance at Rory.

His eyes widen with what I'm sure he thinks is innocence.

I reach in and remove the beautiful silver charm bracelet. There are five charms hanging from the links. The first is a lovely silver crescent moon, next is a little cup of coffee with silver latte art, followed by a stack of miniature books with different colored enamel covers and spines, and next is a miniature cat-eye emerald ring that bears a striking resemblance to one of Rory's previous presents. The final charm is an image of spoiled little Pyewacket, complete with tufted ears and tiny topaz eyes.

"It's beautiful. Where did you get these charms? That one of the cat really looks like Pyewacket."

Rory takes a deep breath before he replies. "In my line of work, you get to know a lot of people in the jewelry business."

Not really an answer, but I'm too impressed to complain. I wrap the bracelet around my left wrist and struggle with the clasp.

Rory turns the wheel to pull off the road, and for a moment I can't breathe. A memory of foster dad number four yanking the steering wheel and driving onto the shoulder hits me like a brick.

A yelp of fear escapes, and I drop the charm bracelet as I throw myself against the door, press my face to the cold glass, and struggle to control my breathing.

"Mitzy, what's wrong? Are you okay? Don't you like the bracelet?"

I press my temples and struggle to push the memory away. I was thirteen and my foster family was driving to visit their cousins in Wickenburg. My foster dad had already given me a long speech about how there wouldn't be any Christmas presents for me, because I wasn't really part of the family. He warned me that if I made any trouble there would be consequences. I'd only lived with this family for three and a half months, prior to the trip, and I'd already suffered those "consequences" seven times. The drive seemed endless, and I guess my "not" brother needed a way to entertain himself. So he started making fun of my easy targets. Calling me names like ghost girl, witch hair, freak face, and finally fat "ash." Not exactly what he said, but that last one got foster dad number four's attention. He blamed the whole incident on me and called me a troublemaker as he reached over the seat and smacked me across the face. The effort of the strike caused him to inadvertently jerk the wheel toward the ditch. The tire caught hard when it hit the gravel and pulled the vehicle with unexpected force. We ended up flying through the ditch, up the embankment, and smashing the headlight on a random fence post. This, of course, was all my fault, and I received the severest "consequences" yet for my thoughtless actions.

A hand gently shakes my shoulder, and my body releases one last spasm of fear before I return to the present. Not the lovely gift-present, just the current mess I've made.

"What happened? Where'd you go?" Rory's concerned face leans toward me, and for a moment my psychic senses tingle and I'm picking up on some latent guilt—not sure if it's mine or his. I push it all away and struggle to retrieve the bracelet from the floor mat.

"I'm super sorry. It's not the bracelet. I love it. It's beautiful." I take a deep breath and continue, "I just had a really weird flashback to something that happened when I was— Never mind. How did you know it was my birthday?"

Rory tilts his head in an adorable puppy-dog way. "I didn't. I just thought a beautiful woman deserved an equally lovely gift. But let me be the first to wish you a Happy Birthday!"

My cheeks flush with warmth and more than a little embarrassment. "Oh. Thank you. My birthday is the first day of spring, March twenty-first."

"Actually, the exact date of the vernal equinox varies each year depending on the precise position of the sun. It can fall anytime between March nineteenth and March twenty-first, in the northern hemisphere." He smiles patronizingly.

I hold up a single finger to silence his lesson. "Let's get something straight. If you're going to be my friend, I'm going to need you to get on board the 'my birthday is always on the first day of spring' train. Got it?"

He winks and nods obediently. "Understood."

I lay the bracelet back across my left wrist, but before I can fumble another attempt at the unique clasp, Rory's strong, artistic fingers reach over the center console and gently pull the ends from my fingers.

I stretch out and touch the gold ring on his pinky finger. "Is this a class ring?"

He pulls his hand back for a moment. "It was my mother's."

Makes sense. I was wondering why someone would order a ring that didn't fit his or her ring finger. Before I can launch into any follow-up questions, he reaches back to my charm bracelet.

He easily clasps the tube-style catch, and I welcome the surge of freedom that washes over me.

Exhaling, I bask in the clean-slate feeling from my head to my toes. I smile warmly at Rory, and my extra senses don't pick up on anything except the lovely twinkle in his green eyes.

"Do you like it?" His hand lingers on mine.

"I really love it. It's amazing and so thoughtful. I can't believe you didn't know it was my birthday. Are you sure someone didn't let it slip?"

"Like who? It's not as though your inner circle has welcomed me with open arms."

"True enough." He has a fair point. I can hardly let him in on the fact that Grams has only recently switched back to team Erick. Regardless, no one would have told him, mostly because no one knows. I suppose Silas would've seen it on some paperwork somewhere, but Grams and Jacob have no idea. I'm so used to pretending I don't have a birthday, so I can avoid disappointment, I completely forgot there are people (and a ghost) who might actually care. "I guess I'll just chalk it up to serendipity." I attempt a flirtatious wink.

He chuckles. "I'm hoping serendipity will agree to be our third wheel all weekend." He grins in that playfully seductive way I can only dream of achieving.

"What do you say we get this rig back on the road and let our winter getaway begin?" I lift my fists in a silent cheer.

My gaze drifts out the window as I ponder our first winter escape, but hopefully not our last. There's something about Rory Bombay, something I can't quite put my finger or any of my extra senses directly on. But nonetheless, there's something.

Rory eases his Land Rover onto the road as I attempt to get a preview of cross-country skiing.

"It's quite easy," he assures me. "You snap the toes of your cross-country ski boots into the ski bindings, and you're ready to go."

In my experience, anything that sounds that easy—isn't. "Sounds a little too good to be true. When did you learn to cross-country ski?"

He laughs for a solid thirty seconds before he replies. "All right, you got me. My first experience with cross-country skiing was not a success. But I persevered, and learned to enjoy it as an activity, rather than a sport."

"You're going to have to elaborate. No story that starts with that big a laugh track can be skipped over."

Rory nods in defeat. "Fair point. I was a sophomore in high school, and I had an unquenchable crush on a senior girl."

I take a deep breath and exhale a long and adolescent "Oooooooo, Rory had a girlfriend."

He shakes his head vigorously. "Not a girlfriend, a crush. She didn't acknowledge my existence. My foolproof plan to join the cross-country team and sit by her on the bus on the drives to our out-of-town meets seemed like a flawless strategy."

"And was it flawless?" I grin and lean toward him with anticipation.

"Oh, it was disastrously flawed. Not only was I a terrible cross-country skier, but I possessed neither the swagger nor the fearlessness required to plunk myself down next to a girl of her caliber in front of an audience of my peers."

One look at the strikingly handsome Rory Bombay and I cannot imagine a girl who could resist him. Clearly he was what is known in the business as a "late bloomer."

"I'll skip over the embarrassing practices and

the broken ski poles, and get straight to the first North Country Cross-Country Roundup with our arch rivals."

A boisterous chuckle escapes before I can clap a hand over my own mouth.

"You're right to laugh." He looks at me and nods in approval. "The captain of the boys cross-country team, a senior who possessed all the qualities I lacked, took the seat beside my dream girl. The entire three-hour bus ride, I got to sit behind them and listen to all of his ridiculous lines, and watch her melt before his onslaught."

Been there. Done that. Don't care to share with Rory.

"By the time we reached the golf course, which had been converted into a cross-country ski competition for the weekend, I was carsick and lovesick. Due to the late arrival of the bus from an all-girls school in the region, it was decided that the boys' race would begin first. The event consisted of two laps around the 2.5-kilometer golf-course track, with participants starting thirty seconds apart. Laps are timed, and your completion time adjusted based on your start time. Cross-country skiing is a well-mannered sport, so if you're in the groomed tracks and a faster skier approaches from behind, they shout 'track,' and you, the slower skier, step off the track to allow the faster participant to continue on."

"Did you get to shout 'track' to anyone?"

"I did not have the pleasure. In fact, so many skiers were shouting 'track' at the back of my head, eventually I simply skied next to the groomed track. When I completed my first lap, one of the time-keepers gestured me toward the finish line, but I was too proud to accept the easy out. I informed her that I had one lap to go, and continued for my second revolution of embarrassment. About halfway through lap number two, a very familiar voice shouted, 'track.'" Rory stops abruptly and shakes his head.

"It wasn't . . . ?" I don't have the heart to finish my question.

"It was." He nods, his eyes heavy with memory. "The girl of my dreams, a talented cross-country and downhill skier, was in the lead of the women's race, which had started, and I spent the last half of my last lap being 'tracked' by all the girls skiing that day."

"Gotta hand it to high school, right?"

He shakes his head and mumbles, "You've no idea."

When we exit the main road, I'm genuinely surprised by the sheer height of the mountain. The road winds through the pine forest and I lean forward with anticipation. As Rory pulls up in front of the Fox Mountain Ski Resort, I'm at a loss for words. The structure is an impressive four stories high and looks as though it was plucked from the Swiss Alps and gently nestled here in almost-Canada. I glance around the parking lot and notice a sparse sprinkling of vehicles.

Rory shuts off the engine and sighs. "For Schloss's sake, I was hoping to see more cars up here. I don't think folks realize all the beauty they can experience this late in the season. There's still plenty of snow cover, but I'm sure we'll see some early boreal flowers peeking through to share their promise of spring."

Slowly I turn and tilt my head. There's a lot to unpack in that touching soliloquy, but I go for the least obvious. "Who's Schloss?"

Rory's gaze drifts lazily over the gingerbread trim surrounding the chalet windows as he turns toward my questioning face. "Ah, yes. Four generations of Schlosses have owned the Fox Mountain Ski Resort. Unfortunately, if they're not able to turn things around and come up with some additional off-season uses for the property, this may be the last generation."

I glance down at my mood ring hoping for a little more information on Fox Mountain or perhaps the Schloss family, but the misty black cabochon shares no secrets with me. Instead, my beautiful new bracelet draws my attention and I gently finger the lovely topaz eyes of the cat charm.

"Are you missing your feline friend already?"

I chuckle. "Hardly. That fiendish feline is more entitled than any young princeling. I can do with a break."

"Well, if you're lucky, you might see one of his distant cousins, a lynx, out on the trail."

I wait for the hairs on the back of my neck to tingle. They do not. "I'm fine with spring flowers if you could let guest services know. I'd like to take the 'no wildlife' track."

We share a chuckle as he opens his door. A gust of wind spirals into the car and I shiver convulsively.

Rory quickly pulls the door closed. "Why don't you get yourself inside the chalet and find the nearest roaring fire. I'll get us checked in and have our bags delivered to the rooms while you order us hot chocolate."

I grab the door handle, but hesitate as a thought pops into my head. "While you check us into our rooms, right? Plural. *Two* rooms."

Rory's green eyes cease to twinkle and he glances down. "I'm a man of my word, Mitzy. I would never stoop to a bait and switch."

Well, now I feel like a horse's behind and will almost certainly do something I regret to try to make up for the comment. "I didn't mean to insult you. And it probably won't help to say that I don't usually date men like you."

The sparkle instantly returns to Rory's eyes and he smiles enticingly. "Date?"

I shrug.

"This weekend is improving already." He grins and hops out of the car.

I zip my coat, pull my stocking hat down over my ears, and make a break for the main entrance, next to a garish maroon-and-gold sign listing the shuttle times.

CHAPTER 5

AFTER SETTLING into our separate rooms, Rory, or possibly a bellhop whom he paid, slips an envelope under my door.

Picking it up, I marvel at the creamy, luxurious texture of the paper. I open the flap and slip out the card. Rory's neat script is familiar to me from his previous grand gestures. The enclosed note invites me to a private dinner at the Top of the Lift as a special guest of Mr. Rory Bombay.

I fan myself with the card and blush.

My goodness, I think that man is either the world's most skilled "player," or my dating life has been sadly lacking for a number of years. I probably don't have to tell you it's most likely one hundred percent the latter.

Looking through the three dresses Grams insisted I pack, I decide to go off script. I choose soft, teal-blue leggings, and an oversized grey cashmere sweater with faux-silver-fox trim. I touch up my makeup and slip on my cozy shearling-lined suede boots.

When the elevator doors open at the first floor, Rory is waiting for me in a lovely pair of European-cut jeans and a thick cable-knit sweater.

Grams would be so proud of my dead-on fashion instincts.

Rory leads the way to the resort bar and, as we scan the room for a table, his phone rings.

He snatches the phone out of his pocket and immediately flicks it to silent, but not before a concerned look passes across his face. "I'm so sorry, Mitzy, but it's an important business call that I really must take. Please order anything you like at the bar and I'll return shortly." Without any further details he turns and hustles out.

I shrug and walk through the alpine-themed bar. Every surface that catches my eye is covered with tole-painted leaves, flowers, and skis. The thick wooden bar top is scarred with age, and my barstool creaks as I take a seat on the thick lambs wool.

Behind the bar, tucked in between the bottles of liquor, are dusty antique lanterns and rusty, long-unused kitchen tools. Logs crackle in one of three fireplaces, and the smell of their warmth lingers in the air.

I glance up and down the somewhat polished surface beneath my elbows, in search of a bar menu. No such luck. As I wave my hand to catch the bartender's attention, a brunette in her late forties approaches and takes the stool next to me.

"I noticed your man left you high and dry. Can I buy you a drink?"

I'm naturally suspicious of strangers, but there's no tingling of the hairs on the back of my neck and no urgent message from my mood ring, so I proceed with caution. "Oh, he just had to take a business call. He'll be back in a minute."

The woman smiles and nods. "Isn't that what they all say." She extends a hand and adds, "I'm Brandy Hammer, the owner of Fox Mountain. And you are?"

I raise my eyebrows and nod. "I'm Mitzy Moon. I own a bookshop in Pin Cherry Harbor. Nice to meet you." We shake hands briefly and she signals the bartender.

He approaches instantly. "What can I do for you Miss—Mrs. Hammer?"

She hesitates for a moment before pasting the smile back on her face. "Get us a couple of hot chocolates, with something special."

The bartender nods and hurries away.

"Is it Miss or Mrs.?" I ask innocently.

She exhales and rubs her finger along one of the timeworn grooves in the bar. "I guess it's both. It was Mrs." She reaches for a glass that is not yet there and instead runs her hand through her shoulder-length brown hair before she answers. "My family has owned this resort for generations, since they came over from Austria and made their fortune in iron ore. My husband Jeffrey and I had planned to run it together until we could pass it down to our daughter. At least that was the plan three years ago when he went for a full-moon ski on his own."

"Is that common?" I ask with a shrug. "I don't know too much about skiing."

She tilts her head back and forth in a noncommittal way. "Normally the moon is so bright and the reflection off the snow so clear that it's perfectly safe. I should probably mention, he might have been drinking a little before he headed out and there was some patchy cloud cover. The fates conspired and, as a thick bank of clouds rolled across the moon, a moose walked out of the tree line. He hit the creature head on and broke his neck. The slope groomer found him in the wee hours and brought his body down the mountain in his snowcat. The ME said Jeffrey died instantly, but who can be sure."

The bizarre story tugs at my heartstrings, and

I understand the pain of losing a loved one. I place a hand on Brandy's shoulder and say the only thing that makes sense at the time. "I lost my mom when I was eleven. It must be very difficult for you."

She looks up, and the vulnerability in her eyes is so raw it brings a lump to my throat.

"It is. Thanks."

The bartender sets down two mugs of what looks like innocent Bavarian hot cocoa, but the burn of alcohol nearly curls my nose hairs as I pick up the cup.

Brandy reaches for a mug and downs half of her heavily spiked hot chocolate before she comes up for air. "My daughter's not handling things well. She's been acting out at school and the principal insisted we—I—get her regular psychiatric care or they'll have to expel her. She's only seven. I probably waited too long to have kids. If I'd had her sooner . . ." Her voice drifts off and she takes another slug of cocoa.

I flick my eyes toward the door and see no sign of Rory. I'm not sure how I got myself into this strangely uncomfortable conversation, but, as much as I feel empathy for her loss, I really don't know this woman and I'm the very last person who should be giving advice on parenting. "At least you'll be able to pass down the resort to her." It's such a lame thing to say, but I literally have nothing else in the tank.

"Not likely." Brandy picks up her mug of hot chocolate and drains it in one long gulp. She slams it down on the bar with surprising force and signals the bartender. "Another round of Sly Foxes for me and my friend."

I catch the barkeep's eye and give him a subtle "no thanks."

Brandy wipes her mouth with the back of her hand and continues to spill her guts. "This old resort has been losing money for years. Once the iron-ore business dried up, we had to make ends meet with just the resort's seasonal income. My husband had a lot of great ideas, and if he was still alive we might've been able to turn things around. But with big corporations looking to open their own resorts, I'm just not sure we can survive the competition."

"I'm sorry to hear that." I risk another glance toward the doorway and a wave of relief washes over me as I see Rory walk through it and smile in my direction. I shrug helplessly as he hurries over.

He stops a couple strides short of me, and a curious, almost irritated, expression pinches his features. "Brandy? Brandy Schloss, is that you?"

The bartender sets down another boozy hot chocolate, but Brandy completely ignores him as she turns toward Rory. "Do I know you?"

From my vantage point, I can see a flash of discomfort scoot across Rory's face before he regains his usual composure. "We've met." He attempts a light-hearted chuckle. "It was a lifetime ago."

Brandy leans back and tilts her head as she stares at Rory. Her bleary eyes don't quite focus.

I wait for a little help from my extra senses, but the awkward silence is killing me. I jump off my stool and step between them. "Brandy Hammer, allow me to introduce Rory Bombay. Mr. Bombay owns an antiquities and artifacts business in Grand Falls."

She twists back and forth on her stool and stares at Rory in disbelief. "Rory Bombay? That wasn't . . . and you didn't have those . . ." Her eyes lap up his striking features.

I can hardly blame her. He is a tall drink of water. But her comments lead me to believe that my suspicion about him being a late bloomer is all too correct. Sadly my lazy mood ring offers no additional confirmation.

Rory slips an arm around my shoulders. "Well, we have a reservation at the Top of the Lift, so we should probably get going. It was lovely to see you, Mrs. Hammer."

As we leave Brandy with her jaw hanging slack, Rory leans down and whispers, "What on earth are you doing talking to her?"

"Oh, she owns this place. And her husband was killed in a terrible skiing accident a few years ago. She saw you abandon me and thought I'd be a sympathetic ear for her troubles, I guess. Apparently, she has a daughter with some behavioral issues as well."

Rory shakes his head. "Was I really gone that long?"

I laugh a little in spite of the seriousness of the situation. "I'm not sure what opened the floodgates. But I think the high-octane hot chocolate might've had something to do with it."

As we approach a rear exit from the lodge, I panic. "I didn't bring my jacket. I didn't know we were going outside."

He turns and smiles at me. "Don't worry, I thought of everything."

A bellhop approaches from a side hallway and wraps me in a thick, heated blanket. He hands a similar one to Rory, and we walk to the base of the ski lift.

We slip into a lift chair and Rory leans toward me as the cables pull us up the mountain.

The moon is rising, and its pearly glow spills out from behind the mountain and pours magically over the snow. The silver-blue trees below us, the crisp clean air, and the twinkling stars tucked into the velvet black sky above make me feel as though I've slipped into a winter wonderland.

The cold breeze rushes across my cheeks and ruffles my hair as the lift trundles up the mountain, but the blissful scenery and the ethereal moonlight seem to warm me from the inside out. At the crest, we slide out of the chair and turn left toward the restaurant instead of right toward the slopes.

A snow-dusted boardwalk guides us to the entrance of Top of the Lift.

The fine-dining establishment reminds me of an old Broadway actress whose glory days are long behind her, yet she still spends hours each morning struggling to keep the march of time at arm's length.

In spite of the dim lighting, the decades of secrets buried in the carpet have been laid bare.

The expected aroma of fabulous food is lost behind a general mustiness, paired with a hint of decay. And the taxidermy black bear in the lobby is missing two claws from his right foot and has several forlorn, hairless patches covering his hide.

Rory pretends to kiss the top of my head as he mumbles, "Apparently, Brandy is not the only thing that has seen better days."

The hostess takes us to our seat and mumbles something unintelligible as she drops our menus onto the table.

"This hardly seems like your type of place, Rory."

He leans back and fixes me with an inscrutable stare. "What would you know about my type of place, Miss Moon?"

"I'm just saying, you strike me as a man who likes his creature comforts. This kind of has-been, crumbling establishment doesn't jive with that classy vibe."

He takes a panoramic inventory and nods sadly. "It used to be booked weeks in advance. In its day, it was one of the finest dining experiences up north. I guess the Schloss family fell on hard times."

I look around. "Clearly."

We get through a dinner, which consists of far too much fondue, and finish with the pleasant surprise of a delicious rhubarb buckle for dessert. A buckle seems to be a cross between a coffee cake and a crumble, but what do I know? The rest of the meal is not really worth mentioning.

Rory escorts me back to my room and promises to meet me in the main dining area for an early breakfast, before my first skiing lesson.

I tippy-toe up and give him a light kiss on the cheek before grumbling my hesitant agreement about early morning *any*things.

CHAPTER 6

Regardless of my misgivings about early mornings, even I have to admit the view from our breakfast table is rather inviting. The sky is powder blue and dotted with cotton-ball clouds, while the sun sparkles through the ice crystals dusting the pine trees.

I think I might actually be feeling a little excited about learning how to ski.

After the requisite number of cups of liquid alert, Rory and I head over to the rental counter.

He ensures that I'm outfitted with the proper-sized skis, boots, poles, and even a helmet.

"A helmet? I'm not that clumsy."

He winks. "It's merely a safety measure, Mitzy, it's not a commentary on your grace."

The rental clerk hands Rory a little map of the

trails, with orange lines indicating the cross-country trails and green, blue, and black indicating downhill ski trails with their corresponding level of difficulty.

We scoop up all our gear and head out to the deck to get suited up. I can't wait to tell Grams that there's not a single human on the slopes wearing knee-breeches.

"Cross-country ski boots are very different from downhill," Rory explains. "With cross-country skiing you need to be able to move your ankle to get your full glide."

We step out onto the packed snow and he shows me how to clip the toe of my ski shoes into the binding of my skis. He also demonstrates how to poke the tip of my ski pole into the spot that detaches the boot, if necessary.

My first lesson is simply walking—in skis—which seems easy enough. Rory sets a very gentle pace and I manage to scoot-slide my way along after him. Once we leave the main slope in front of the resort, the single set of parallel tracks in the snow is the only indication that any human has been in this wilderness before us. The snow is white and glistening, and the trees hug close to the sides of the trail.

Rory stops suddenly and I slide right over his skis.

"I suppose I should've given at least one lesson on stopping," he whispers.

"Hindsight is twenty-twenty, right?" I match his quiet tone, afraid to disturb the pristine, silver-white landscape.

Rory steps off the trail and gestures for me to slide up next to him. About a hundred yards ahead of us, to the side of the trail, is a large buck.

"That looks like an eight-point buck, or a western four-point."

He nods. "Impressive. Where did you learn so much about deer?"

"Oh, that's the full extent of my knowledge. We had deer in Arizona, and one of my foster dads grew up in South Dakota. So, I know various parts of the country count points differently on antlers, and that's pretty much it."

Rory laughs, and the deer leaps into the cover of the trees.

He gives me a quick lesson on something called "snowplowing," which involves angling my skis in a strange "V" shape, in case I need to stop in the future. Then we continue along the trail. At our next stop, I manage to shove my poles into the snow and prevent my forward progress, just shy of crashing into Rory a second time.

"Still working on that snowplow move," I joke.

He smiles and steps off the trail to show me a

lovely little flower peeking through the snow. “This is a trillium. You rarely see them blooming this early, but doesn’t it look beautiful framed against the snow?”

I gaze at the three, pointed, green leaves framing three pure-white petals and nod my agreement. “It’s beautiful.”

Thirty minutes, or more, down the trail we see another flower, which looks very similar, but Rory assures me that it is a sharp-lobed hepatica bud, and that when it opens it will have six petals, rather than three, like the trillium.

Our next visual treat is a tufted-eared lynx, which reminds me of my dear spoiled Pyewacket and brings a surge of warm tingles to my heart. The welcome distraction nearly makes me forget the fatigue seeping into my limbs.

“There’s a bit of a downhill up ahead. Don’t be afraid if you pick up speed. Keep your weight evenly distributed over each ski, and bend your knees a little. Just ride it out with your skis side by side, like french fries. The slope levels at the bottom and turns ever so slightly to the left. You’ll do fine.”

I wish I felt as confident as Rory sounds. However, I’m pretty much a french fry expert, so how bad can it be?

“Wait here, watch me, and do the same.” Rory sticks his poles in and gives himself a solid launch onto the hill. He glides down with glorious ease and leans effortlessly to the left to make the curve. He comes to a stop, jump turns, and waves a ski pole in a gesture that must mean for me to follow.

I choose to avoid the launch, and instead allow the slow decline to control my pace.

Surprisingly, I'm still upright and feeling a morsel of confidence. I see the left turn approaching and that's when panic sets in. I don't know what to do with my poles—and now I've forgotten everything Rory said. Instead of gently rolling left as he did, I careen straight ahead, off the trail, toward the trees, and begin flailing my poles in a panic.

The flailing motion helps me avoid a pine, but my attempt to snowplow causes me to veer hard to the right and catch a ski tip on a small birch tree. I fly headlong into an unusually firm snowbank.

Stinging from both embarrassment and the icy snow covering my face, I attempt to recover a little dignity with some self-deprecating humor. "Looks like the helmet was a solid plan." I wipe my face with a cold, wet mitten. "That snowbank was pretty solid."

Rory roughly pulls me back toward the trail, skis flopping and scraping along behind.

I jerk free of his grasp. "Hey, what are you doing?"

His eyes have lost all their sparkle and his skin

has a deathly pallor. "That's no snowbank." He gestures weakly toward my crash site.

Following the motion, and without any warning from my special senses, or my ring, I find myself staring at red streaks in the snow, a frozen hand, and the body that goes with it.

I'm certain my eyes must be playing tricks on me. Maybe I have snow blindness, or I'm hallucinating. "That's not a body, is it?" I look to Rory, hoping he'll explain how I hit my head and it's not a hand, but some other early-spring flower.

Instead, he unclips from his skis and swallows hard. "It's definitely a body. Call for help while I check for identification."

Turning, I watch him cautiously approach the corpse. The sound of his feet crunching in the snow is louder than an avalanche in my ears. I rub my eyes repeatedly, but the image refuses to disappear. Taking off my mitten, I cover my mouth and stare as Rory kneels down and gently brushes away the snow.

Then reality hits me like a speeding locomotive—right in the gut. I scoot-ski to a nearby tree and grab it with one hand while unloading my breakfast into the scant underbrush. I pick up a handful of snow to wash the sick from my face. Taking several deep breaths, I struggle to convince my stomach to calm down.

I'm too weak to figure out how to turn around on these infernal skis. It would be great to get them off my feet, but I have no idea where I dropped my poles. So, I begin scoot-skiing backward until I feel a hand on my shoulder. I jump involuntarily.

"It's all right, Mitzy, it's only me."

Leaning into the firm hand, I take a ragged breath.

His voice is quiet and soothing. "Did you call the authorities?"

I can't remember how to talk. So I shake my head and blink back tears.

Rory extends his hand. "There's no identification, no phone, just this weird recording device."

Regardless of the horrible situation, my curiosity gets the best of me. I turn and look at the item in his hand. As a film-school dropout, I instantly recognize it and find a whisper of my voice. "That's not a recording device, that's a light meter. Photographers and filmmakers use them to make sure they get the right exposure for the shot. That guy's gotta be one or the other. And a professional. No amateur would be carrying around an expensive piece of equipment like that."

Rory turns the device over in his hand and asks, "Should I call?"

I nod.

He hands me the light meter and retrieves his

phone out of the zippered inner pocket of his jacket.

While he calls in our horrible discovery, I turn on the light meter and make a mental note of the last reading: f/1.4/800. In case you're not a photography buff, that's a very large aperture and a fast shutter speed. Usually indicates low lighting. My first assumption would've been somewhere inside with relatively little ambient light, but since we found *IT* out here, it makes me wonder if there was some kind of night shoot. I shuffle around the area, not too close to the *thing* in the snow, but I don't see a tripod or any sign of camera equipment. Maybe it was a robbery?

"The deputy told us to wait here until the ski patrol arrives to secure the scene." He puts his phone away and zips his pocket.

I scoot toward him. "Deputy? You mean the ski resort is in the sheriff's jurisdiction?"

Rory nods affirmatively, but his eyes widen in surprise. "I thought you were well-acquainted with the sheriff. All of Birch County is his jurisdiction."

I let out a low whistle and reply, "I had no idea. I never really gave it much thought."

Rory mumbles, just loud enough for me to hear, "It appears Sheriff Harper gives it enough thought for both of you."

The old rivalry resurfaces. Not that there's really anything going on between Erick and I, but I have to admit, from Rory's perspective we do tend to run into Sheriff Too-Hot-To-Handle too often to be entirely accidental.

As the initial surge of terror-induced adrenaline subsides, the muscle-ache and frosty tingling in my extremities can no longer be ignored. "I'm freezing. Did they say how long the ski—" The sound of schussing, which I never really understood until this very moment, interrupts my complaint. Three red-jacket-clad skiers spin jump to a stop just off the trail. Their redheaded leader pushes his goggles up onto his stocking hat. "You the ones that found the body?"

I put a hand on my stomach as it swirls with a queasy threat.

"Yes. I'm Rory Bombay and this is Mitzy Moon. We're guests at the lodge and we were out for a little nature ski."

The leader of the patrol nods. "We'll take it from here. You can return to the lodge."

For some reason, I shove the light meter in my pocket and call out to Rory to prevent him from revealing that part of our find. "Rory, can you get my poles and help me out of here?"

He clips back into his skis, collects all of our poles, and even my discarded mitten.

"Thanks." I take the poles and slowly make a fifteen-point turn back toward the trail.

Rory leans in and whispers, "You don't want to tell them about the light meter?"

"I prefer to hand it directly to Sheriff Harper."

A flash of irritation passes over Rory's face. "Of course."

Snuggled under a thick blanket, with a boozy hot chocolate and a roaring fire, I'm beginning to feel almost normal.

I'm the first to see Erick approaching, but intentionally avert my gaze and pretend to be entranced by the flames.

"When the lady at the front desk said that I could find the skiers who discovered the body in the fireplace room, I should've known it would be you, Miss Moon."

Not to be outdone, Rory retorts, "And I should've known it would be you, Sheriff Harper."

Erick ignores Rory's comment and gets straight down to business. "The remains were recently disturbed. Can I assume that was your doing as well?"

Cut to—me setting down my mug of hot chocolate and standing defiantly. "For your information, Erick, he was already dead when I crashed into him."

Erick jerks his head back as though I slapped him across the face. "I wasn't implying that you had anything to do with the death, I just need your statements."

I put a fist on one of my ample hips. "You'll have to excuse me for being proactively defensive. It wouldn't be the first time you've accused me of murder, Erick."

He glances back and forth between Rory and me and makes a statement, not a question. "So, the two of you were up here for a ski weekend, and just happened to find the body. You really do seem to be a magnet for corpses, Miss Moon."

"Rude." I could explain how Rory won the trip at a fundraiser and how we have separate rooms, but I'm currently a little miffed at Erick and actually enjoy watching him stew in his own juices. "I'm learning how to cross-country ski. That was my first turn of the day and I couldn't quite get my skis sorted out. I kind of crash-landed into the body." I can tell you right now, I don't appreciate the ease of Erick's laughter. I mean, I'm not that clumsy.

"Was there any identification on the body?"

Rory's sulking, monotone voice answers the query. "There was not."

"Anything else noteworthy?"

I toy with the idea of letting things play out for

a few more minutes, but I have no interest in impeding the investigation. "There was a light meter."

Erick's pen pauses above his notepad. "What?"

I grab my jacket off the end of the sofa and fish around in the pocket. "Here. It's a light meter. Photographers and filmmakers use them to make sure they get the right exposure."

"Why did you remove evidence from the scene?"

"Rory was looking for identification and found this. Most people don't know what it is, so I wanted to give it to you myself."

"You'd be surprised how many cases we solved before you moved to Pin Cherry Harbor, Miss Moon." Erick pulls an evidence bag from his pocket and holds it open.

I drop the light meter into the bag and decide to keep my theory about the possible night-shoot to myself, since Sheriff Harper is acting so high and mighty. "Copy that."

"About what time would you say you discovered the body?"

"Not more than a couple of minutes before the 9-1-1 call, Sheriff." Rory's voice has softened, but he refuses to make eye contact with Erick.

"If you need anything else, you can contact my lawyer." I sit back down on the deep leather sofa, too close to Rory for even my own comfort.

The muscles in Erick's jaw tighten and he slips his notepad and pen away. "We may have additional questions after the ME completes her examination. You'll be back in Pin Cherry Harbor tomorrow?"

Rory slips his right arm around my shoulders and for the first time looks directly at Erick. "We'll see how the rest of our weekend unfolds, Sheriff."

Erick nods curtly and stalks out of the fireplace room.

I punch Rory, half-playfully/half-menacingly, on the arm. "That was mean."

"It was. But I won't apologize. That man is always showing up at the worst possible time. You'll indulge me a moment of vindictiveness, won't you?" Rory strokes my cheek with one long graceful finger and leans toward me.

I'm suddenly not sure if I'm ready for this. The hairs on the back of my neck might not be tingling, but my tummy sure is. My eyelids flutter and my mouth softens.

He's so close now. I can feel his cocoa-scented breath on my face. He scoops his hand into my hair.

I close my eyes.

"There's one more thing, Miss Moon."

My eyelids flip open like spring-roller window shades on an old train, and my cheeks blush crimson. "And what could that possibly be, Erick?"

"Did you find the light meter on the body of the victim, or somewhere else at the scene?"

Am I actually hearing a hint of jealousy in Erick's tone? And his question seems highly mundane and not at all urgent. "Rory? I believe you'll have to answer that."

Rory leans back with an exaggerated exhale of irritation. "The light meter was in the victim's left coat pocket. The pocket was zipped. I searched for some form of identification, but I found only the light meter. Nothing else. Not a single thing." He glares at Erick.

All I can think is, *if looks could kill . . .* However, Erick does seem to be sporting an overly smug grin, which deflects the power of Rory's deadly stare.

"All right, boys, it's been a long day for all of us. Erick, you should get that evidence back to the lab. You know how to reach me if you have any additional questions." I cross my arms and add, "You've always known how to reach me."

Rory gives me a suspicious side-eye, while I take my turn glaring at the sheriff.

I sincerely hope Erick receives the double meaning of my statement. I happen to be here on a ski weekend with Rory because Rory asked. If Erick had wanted to take me on a ski weekend, or anywhere for that matter, he could've used his words.

CHAPTER 7

Despite my exhausting day and my high-octane Sly Fox in the fireplace room, I can't fall asleep. I'm just lying on my hotel bed—alone, in case anyone was wondering—and every time I shut my eyes, I see the body in the snow. I flip from one side to the other and the topaz stones in my Pyewacket charm catch the moonlight peeking through my curtains. I rub the little charm between my fingers and hope it will bring me sleep.

No such luck.

Rolling out of bed, I slip a thick sweater over my "Time to Make the Biscuits" T-shirt, featuring a cat in a chef's hat. I pull a pair of jeans on over my leggings and shove my feet into my warm snow boots, while searching for my room key.

And I do mean key, not a swipe card, not any

sort of modern technology. Much like the type-writers at my bank and the slidey credit card machine at my dry cleaner, the Fox Mountain Ski Resort uses good old-fashioned metal keys.

I slip some cash in my pocket and head out of my room, expecting empty hallways, closed bars, and more disappointment than distraction.

I'm alone in the hallway. I'm alone in the elevator. I'm alone as I traipse through the lobby and inspect the rotting stuffed mammals and birds that attempt to camouflage the peeling paint on the walls. As I approach the hallway between the main desk and the bar, raised voices echo through the emptiness. I duck behind a fake ficus, and listen with my whole body.

The voices sound female.

One is angry and the other scared.

One of the voices sounds like Brandy, and it seems like a typical employee/employer argument. Trust me, I've had more than my share. I'm about to continue my search for entertainment when one of the voices growls, "Body."

Uh oh. You have my attention, faceless arguers.

They lower their voices and I don't catch a name, but I catch the word "missing." Suddenly, the voice that I'm sure belongs to Brandy Hammer slurs drunkenly, "Jus' keep th'cops out of room 237."

Time to disappear.

I hustle down a hallway that dead-ends at an ice machine and vending machine. I have no ice bucket, but I think I have a dollar bill. I feed it into the vending machine and push any button.

A lumbering, rolling sound that lasts far too long is followed by the thundering deposit of a can of Tab in the exit bin.

Bending down like an archaeologist on an important dig, I extract the find. Speaking to no one but myself, I narrate my discovery. "We think the people suffered from a severe lack of taste. There may also have been some geographical difficulties involved in their limited beverage selections. But we are confident that this is the last remaining original can of Tab."

Chuckling to myself, I walk down the hallway and pop the top open on the can.

The maid's cart is parked outside a room that says "Laundry," and her shiny little ring of keys is calling my name like a possessed doll in an episode of *Twilight Zone.*

I swallow hard, glance behind and ahead, snag the keys and shove them into my back pocket as I speed-walk back to the elevator. I have a sudden need to see what they're keeping from the police in room 237.

Brandy is stumbling across the foyer with her phone in one hand and the other stretched out to her side in an attempt to avert a possible fall. She's nearly on the other side of the large open space, and the last thing I want to do is attract her attention. But I can't very well stand here in the hallway until the maid comes back and finds her keys are missing.

So, I attempt to walk as quietly as I imagine a ballerina would toward the elevator. I'm reaching out to push the "up" button and I breathe a sigh of relief, completely forgetting that elevators always announce their arrival with a nice loud—

BONG!

"Mitzy? Is that you?"

I know it's rude, but she's extremely drunk and I feel certain she won't remember this in the morning. Admittedly, I do have some experience in this area. "Hey, Brandy, I'm exhausted. I'll see you for breakfast," I say as the elevator doors shut.

I push "four" in case she's watching the lights, and exit on the fourth floor, but I don't return to my room. Instead, I hurry to the stairwell, which smells of stale cigarette smoke, and run down two flights.

Easing open the door on the second floor, I take a peek both ways. The hallway is empty. So I hurry toward room 237 and pray to anything and everything that's listening that no one comes out of their room while I attempt to find the right master key.

Ignoring the "Do Not Disturb" sign, I begin my

hunt. Luck is on my side, and the third key I test slips in and easily opens the door.

You know that scene in every movie when they go to search the room, or the apartment, or the house, and they leave the door open behind them? I don't do that. I close the door. Throw the deadbolt. And lock the chain. Nobody's gonna surprise me.

First item of note: whoever is staying in this room is a filthy pig. Empty chip bags and candy bar wrappers litter the floor. And I count at least six Tab cans in the trash. I'm tempted to launch into another archaeology narration, but I really don't have time. What I need to find is some connection between this empty room and the—ew—body.

Step 1: Check the safe. It's open.

Step 2: Check the fridge. Indescribable odors.

Step 3: Closet. Filled with smelly clothes. Disgusting.

Under the bed. Nothing.

The bureau drawers hold more clothes and a notebook.

Eureka! "Property of Oliver Kedrowski" is printed on the cover. Inside, the first number scratched on the page is for the features editor at the *Tribune Times*.

And there's my connection. Light meter. *Tribune Times*.

I close the notebook and replace it in the

drawer. This guy wasn't just a photographer. He was a photojournalist with the *Tribune Times*.

Now, I haven't lived in almost-Canada all that long, but I've actually heard of that paper, so I have to believe it's kind of a big deal. Also, if he had the number written down, he hadn't worked there very long. Maybe he was freelancing?

Better finish my search and get out of here. My eyes dart to the clock on the nightstand. It can't really be five in the morning. That's not right. All right, time to focus.

I check the rest of the drawers and the bedside table. I will not tell you what I find in there. It's not helpful to my investigation. As I try to slide the drawer back in, something catches and I freeze in my tracks.

Of course! Finally a movie trope that does not disappoint.

I pull out the drawer, tip it upside down, and there on the bottom of the drawer . . . Oliver taped an SD card from his camera.

I scowl at my useless mood ring, rip the card and tape off the back, and shove them into my pocket.

Now I just need to drop these keys in the hallway somewhere and get back to my room. I take two steps toward the door and hear thundering boot-falls in the hallway. What are the odds that—

A key slips in the lock.

My heart stops beating.

I have to jump. I step to the window, slide back the curtain, and struggle to ignore the pounding on the door to room 237.

Oh, glorious! It's a hand-crank window. I crank as fast as I can, while keeping my eye on the door as the banging and key twisting continues. I'm sure they can hear the creaking of this stupid ancient pane of glass inching open.

Once it's finally wide enough, I launch through the screen, out the window, and instantly land in the snow. I was all prepared for a ten to twelve foot drop, but apparently the chalet is built into the hill-side and the second-floor windows, at the back, just step right out into the snow.

No time to complain about architecture. I'm alive and I'm running.

Of course, running is absolutely the most suspi-cious behavior I could perform at this time. So I at-tempt to control my breathing and slow to what should appear to be a leisurely early-morning pace.

I feel my back pocket for the keys and panic.

Where are the keys?

I dropped them somewhere. Either in the room or in the snow.

There's no going back.

I slip around the corner and glance toward the

entrance. As I suspected, a black-and-white cruiser, lights spinning, sits directly in front of the lodge.

While I ponder my next move and calculate how long until I'm arrested, a glorious sight rolls into view.

The shuttle. The shuttle!

I jog toward the road, slip in the snow and nearly land in front of the bus, but manage to slide to a stop waving my arms.

The shuttle driver skids to a halt and opens the door. "This is the express back to Pin Cherry."

"Exactly what I'm looking for." I step on board and collapse into the first seat.

"Pickups and drop-offs at the main bus terminal on Gunnison, and a special Sunday morning stop at Myrtle's Diner."

I lean back against the seat and exhale.

Someone, I'm guessing Grams, is really watching out for me today. I lean my head against the cool window. Before I know it, the bus driver is shaking me awake.

"Miss, Miss. This is the end of the line, eh. You want to go back to the ski resort? I thought you said you were headed to Pin Cherry."

I lean forward and rub my eyes in a daze.

The events of the past twenty-four hours rush back into my consciousness like a horrible montage.

I turn to look out the window of the bus and I see a magnificent sign. Pun intended.

"Myrtle's Diner. Open."

I smile at the driver and hand him all the cash in my pocket. "I hope this is enough. I can't thank you . . ." I stumble off the bus, marveling at my lack of linguistic capability.

Pushing my way into the diner, I grin like a Cheshire cat.

CHAPTER 8

The blessed warmth of my home-away-from-home envelops me, and for the first time in a couple of days, I let my guard down.

Odell gives me a spatula salute through the orders-up window, and I take a seat at the counter.

Tally's flame-red bun looks freshly dyed, and she gives me a conspiratorial wink as she slides a cup of coffee in front of me. "Are you back early from your special weekend?"

"You'd be surprised how a dead body tends to put a dampener on things."

Her eyes widen to saucers, and Odell strides out from the kitchen.

I take a careful sip from my steaming mug of black gold and enjoy keeping my audience on the edge of their metaphorical seats.

Odell has no time for such things. “Are you gonna spill the beans, kid? Or should I let your breakfast burn?”

I chuckle as I set down my cup. “It’ll certainly be in tomorrow’s paper. They found a body out on Fox Mountain.”

Tally puts a hand over her mouth and scurries away.

Odell leans toward me. “And when you say ‘they,’ do you mean you?”

I glance around the diner at the smattering of early-morning eaters and lower my voice. “I need to talk to you, privately.”

“We’ll head out back when you finish your breakfast.” He raps his knuckles twice on the counter and returns to the grill.

I power through my breakfast, thankful it’s not fondue, and bus my dishes into the bin under the counter when I finish.

It’s amazing what a few months can do. I remember the day I first stepped off the bus in Pin Cherry Harbor and walked into Myrtle’s Diner to the utter shock and awe of the locals. Now this place feels like a second home, and Odell is the kind but curmudgeonly grandfather I never had.

Odell gives a little shout to let Tally know he’s on a break, and we step through the back door of the kitchen into the alley.

I glance down at the cigarette in his pocket and I'm surprised to see that it's fresh and new, rather than the tattered old smoke I'm used to seeing. "Did you start smoking again?"

His expression is a mixture of shock and confusion. He glances down and pulls the cigarette from his pocket. "Nah. But I have to replace the token every few years. It's been almost sixteen years since my mother died of cancer, and Walt and I took that as our cue to stop smoking. The doctor swore it would prolong our lives." Odell's eyes drift off into the distance in a cloud of dark memories. "I guess it worked out for one of us."

"So sorry about Walt. I'm sure he was a good guy."

"Well, nothing I can do about that now. What can I do for you?"

"There's a chance I may have gotten myself into a little entering but not breaking, some light theft of evidence, and perhaps a smidge of breaking and exiting."

Odell lets out a long whistle. "It's like standing in the presence of Myrtle Isadora all over again." He chuckles as he places the cigarette between his lips.

He never lights it, of course. He told me once it was just a symbol of what he overcame and a reminder of his willpower.

"So, like you said, I was the one who found the body. And I'm pretty sure I know who it is."

Odell nods and gestures for me to continue.

"I searched his room and I think the body we found is Oliver Kedrowski, a photojournalist for the *Tribune Times*."

Odell tilts his head. "Searched his room?"

I filled him in on the details of the body, the aperture reading from the light meter, the argument I overheard, and my escape from Fox Mountain with the stolen evidence."

"And what do you need from me?"

I shiver. "I don't know. I guess I need you to tell me I'm not crazy."

"Let's finish this conversation inside." Odell slips the cigarette back in the breast pocket of his faded-blue shirt and we return to the snug kitchen.

"Maybe I should get back to the bookshop to see what's on this card."

"You know your grandmother would be awful proud of you. I'd give my right arm to let her have five minutes with you." His eyes fill with emotion and he busies himself at the grill.

I wish I could tell him. I wish I could let him in on the little magical blessing that is my Ghost-ma. But she and I agree that it would only bring him further heartache to know that her spirit still roams the earth and he has no way to communicate with her. I put a hand on his shoulder and give it a little squeeze. "At least I've got you."

He nods and covers his emotion with gruffness. "Free burgers and fries for life. At least you got that."

Smiling, I thank Tally for the excellent service and jog briskly back to my bookshop.

Fishing my special key from the chain around my neck, I slip it in the lock, twist it three times, and listen to the tumblers clicking into place. I would've thought Grams would be eagerly waiting for me on the other side, but I don't sense her presence.

Opening the door, I step into the store, shivering as a chill grips my body. I guess running around in the winter without a jacket isn't such a great plan. I'll worry about getting my stuff from the lodge later; right now, I need to see what's on this SD card. "Grams? Grams?"

Nothing.

Well, it wouldn't be the first time I've had to go searching for her. She gets caught up in her little projects and exercises, and apparently forgets all about me.

Pyewacket bounds down the wrought-iron spiral staircase and meows.

Strange. I don't get what he's saying. Admittedly, when I first moved here, I didn't really understand him either. But it only took me a couple days to figure out what he really wanted and recognize the differences in his vocalizations.

For some reason, today he just sounds like a normal cat.

Rushing upstairs, I cross the Rare Books Loft and pull the candle handle next to the empty shelf where *Saducismus Triumphatus* used to be.

With all the dead-body nonsense, I completely forgot to confront Rory about my missing tome. I suppose I'll have plenty of time for that later. "Grams? Grams, where the heck are you?"

The bookcase door slides open and I prepare to be surprised by the sudden appearance of Ghost-ma.

Nothing.

I search through the apartment and feel another terrible chill as I walk back into the loft. The bookcase door slides closed behind and I still haven't located Grams.

Heading into the back room, I pour a bowl of Fruity Puffs for Pyewacket. He meows again and rubs against my leg. But I still don't get what he's trying to say.

Time to check the museum. Grams has an affinity for the third floor. I pass through the "Employees Only" door separating my bookshop from the printing museum, wind my way through the lovely antique printing presses and climb the stairs to the third floor. Another shiver grips my body and I'm surprised by how cold it is in the museum. "Grams? Grams, I'm running out of options! Where are you?"

A terrible chill grips me and goosebumps cover my arms.

Wait— "Grams?"

Since my first day in Pin Cherry Harbor, when the ghost of my grandmother scared the bejeezus out of me with her sudden appearance in the apartment, I've never gotten ghost-chills. I've always been able to see her and talk to her. Only the people who can't see her or talk to her get ghost-chills.

I feel a sick heaviness in my stomach and a solid lump in my throat.

What if she's here and I can't see her?

A stack of papers falls to the floor.

"Grams? Is that you?"

A quill pen falls to the floor.

"Grams, I can't see you. I can't see you at all. What's happening?"

A pen floats out of its holder and I watch with increasing terror as it scratches out a message on a piece of paper.

If I thought seeing a ghost was frightening, not seeing one is the absolute worst. I look down at the paper and read, "Mitzy, I'm right here. I haven't gone anywhere. Why can't you see me?"

"I don't know what's happening. Grams, I can't see you. I can't hear you. I can't even understand Pyewacket."

Collapsing into a chair, I sob into the arm of my sweater. Everything about my life and Pin Cherry Harbor is falling apart. The wonderful family I discovered here and the feeling of safety and love in this bookshop—it's gone.

The bookstore feels like an empty mausoleum.

And just like that, I'm orphan Mitzy all over again.

A ghostly touch shakes my shoulder and I jerk away in fright.

The phantom-wielded pen scratches out another message from beyond. "Mizithra Achelois Moon! Get a hold of yourself! Call Silas immediately!"

I wipe my tears and nod obediently. "That's a lot of exclamation points, Grams."

I wish I could hear her laughter . . .

Fishing my phone out of my pocket, I call my lawyer and mentor. I flick the speaker on so Grams can hear him even if I can't hear her.

"Good morning, Mitzy. How might you be?"

"I know you're always saying how important manners are, Silas, but I have a real emergency and I'm too panicked to care. I can't see Grams. I can't talk to her, and I don't even understand Pyewacket.

I need you —" Another round of sobs shakes my shoulders and I drop the phone onto the display table.

"I shall be there posthaste." The call ends

Glancing around the room, I search high and low for any tiny shimmer or disturbance that could possibly be a sign of Grams.

Still nothing. Pyewacket has somehow found us and rubs his head roughly against my leg. I bend to scratch him between his black-tufted ears and he hisses at me threateningly.

Yanking my hand back in shock, I whisper, "Pye, it's me. It's Mitzy. Don't you recognize me?" I cautiously reach toward him with my left hand and he takes an angry thwack at my wrist.

Time seems to slow down, rewind, and then play in slow-motion.

The gold box.

Strange feelings.

The bracelet locking around my wrist.

That inexplicable feeling of freedom.

But it wasn't freedom. It was something so much darker.

I struggle with the clasp, but to no avail. There's just no way to unhook it. I yank and tug and pull, but the thing must be made out of titanium! I can't get it off my wrist.

Chills keep shooting down my spine, so I can

only assume that Grams is swirling around me in a frantic effort to offer some kind of help.

The pen scratches across the page, "Who gave you that bracelet?"

Even though I can't hear her, I'm sure she's still busily reading my thoughts. I'm powerless to keep Rory's name from my mind.

A chair tips over and I know, even without my extrasensory perceptions, that Grams is furious.

"I'm gonna go downstairs and wait for Silas. Don't be mad, Grams. Please don't be mad."

I rush downstairs and into the bookshop before she can take any otherworldly vengeance.

Hurrying into the back room, I search the drawers for a pair of pliers or a wire cutter.

Nada. Bupkus.

I continue to tug, pull, and twist at the bracelet until my left wrist is red and sore.

When the front door finally opens, I'm frantic and more than a little unhinged.

"Silas! Finally."

"Return to the back room and be seated."

The air around me stirs and I walk backwards, unsure whether the movement is a choice or compulsion.

Silas follows at a distance and his eyes never look directly into mine.

Once I've taken a seat, as instructed, my heart

begins to race. "I can't get the bracelet off. I'm sure it's the bracelet. I never should've put it on. I know you and Grams warned me about Rory. But he was so kind . . . And all the presents—"

"Quiet." The commanding voice of my alchemist-attorney brings a heavy silence to the room.

A chill passes through me and I know Grams must be nearby. Little salty tears trickle down my cheeks.

Silas takes a small brown glass vial out of some hidden interior pocket in his shabby tweed coat. He sets the vial on the table, adjusts his bowtie, and harrumphs into his mustache. "You mentioned that you can no longer see Isadora. Are there any other symptoms?"

Sniffling loudly, I once again replay the events of the weekend, and finally notice all the red flags I blissfully ignored. "I haven't gotten any messages, visions, or feelings since I put this thing on."

Silas traces a series of symbols in the air between us. "I fear the bracelet is simply a modern interpretation of a witch's bottle. Whether it is through an incantation or its construction, the bracelet has effectively captured your powers."

"Why? No one but you and—" I choke back a sob "—Grams know that I even have these powers."

Silas reaches into another hidden pocket and pulls out his bespelled spectacles. He hooks the wire arms behind his ears and his eyes appear comically enlarged through the pink-tinted lenses. He gazes toward a spot over my right shoulder. "Isadora, we initially accepted Mr. Bombay's explanation that he had no idea that his original gift, the emerald ring, was cursed."

I assume she must be nodding in agreement, but I can't hold my tongue. "But I never told Rory how the ring affected me. I just made up that story about being sick because of the undercover gig at the high school and all the germs or something. He totally bought the story, and I wore the ring when he took me out for that fancy dinner. For all he knew, it had no affect on me."

Silas strokes his mustache with his thumb and forefinger. "Perhaps. However, Mr. Bombay is well acquainted with my alchemical studies and the depth of my arcane knowledge. He may have suspected I was able to break the curse."

"What purpose would he have to cut me off from my powers?"

Silas lifts his chin and seems to be chewing on his mustache, but I can't take my eyes off his wagging jowls.

"Can you get this thing off me or not?"

"Let me address your previous query. He may have chosen to interrupt your powers for the simple purpose of having a normal weekend. Unfortunately, I feel the truth will reveal a more sinister purpose."

Silas looks over my right shoulder again and his eyes go wide with shock.

"What? What did Grams do?"

Silas exhales and shakes his head. "I shall repeat neither the gesture nor the implication."

I turn and look over my right shoulder, hoping to catch a glimpse, but the emptiness almost breaks my heart. Based on my knowledge of my grandmother's laundry list of ex-husbands and special friends, I'm sure I can come up with a fairly accurate guess at her implication, even without my powers. "I realize I didn't have the advantage of my psychic senses, but Rory was a perfect gentleman all weekend. We had separate rooms and he never even tried so much as—"

Silas leans toward me. "As what?"

"Well, I was going to say 'a kiss.' But there was a moment in the fireplace room, right before Erick interrupted us."

Silas chuckles in spite of the heavy mood in the room. "Good man. Now, let's see if I can remove this bracelet."

I lay my wrist on the table and swallow audibly. "Will it hurt?"

Silas uncorks the tiny vessel and peers into the neck of brown glass. "I would like to think it will be a painless sublimation, but this will be my first attempt to remove a witch-bottle-turned-bracelet. Let us all hope for the best."

I feel a chill and shiver violently.

Silas looks up through his rose-colored glasses. "Isadora, you must move away from Mitzy. There's no telling how the philosopher's salt could affect a tethered spirit."

The chill against the back of my neck vanishes, and Silas replaces his spectacles in his inner pocket. He pours a small mound of what he called "philosopher's salt" into the palm of his right hand and proceeds to trace a series of symbols into the crystals. Then he closes his fist and moves it toward the bracelet. He tilts his hand and, with a strange swirling motion of his pinky finger, he releases the philosopher's salt—one grain at a time.

The swirling stream of granules is mesmerizing, but it's nothing compared to the strange static electricity that pulls them toward the metal. As the grains fall, they create a coating around the clasp—layer upon layer, like the scales of a dragon.

I can't tell you how much time passes. I'm completely entranced by the fluttering, clinging crystals.

When his hand is empty Silas places two fingers on top of the clasp and whispers, "Recludo, retego, aperio."

He then slips his thumb under the clasp and pinches it between his thumb and forefinger. The metal turns to dust—or maybe a vapor—and a little puff of grey flashes from his fingers as the bracelet falls to the table.

I gasp for air, and immediately search the room for Grams.

No need to look far. She hurtles toward me like a phantom rocket and wraps her ethereal arms around me.

I can't stop crying long enough to say anything, so I just accept my ghost hug like the crying little orphan that I am and wait for someone else to say something.

"Ree-ow." I told you so.

Happy laughter spills forth and I have to give Pyewacket credit where credit is due. "You're right, Robin Pyewacket Goodfellow, you did tell me to take off the bracelet. I just couldn't understand you, Mr. Cuddlekins."

Pyewacket saunters over and swirls a figure eight around my legs while Grams continues to squeeze her arms around me.

Silas puts the stopper back in his bottle, slips it inside his marvelous tweed coat, and turns away to hide his emotion.

I collapse back into the chair and take a ragged

breath. "I never thought I'd be so happy to see a ghost in my whole life!"

"You know things are bad when you've scared a ghost, sweetie. When you couldn't see or hear me, I felt like I really had died. It was the first time since I watched my own funeral that I thought I might've made a mistake."

I scrunch up my face and look at Grams. "What do you mean saw your own funeral? I thought you were tethered to the bookshop."

A hearty chuckle from Silas draws my attention. "Your grandmother included very specific instructions for her funeral in her last wishes. Among those instructions was the stipulation that the memorial service must be conducted at the bookshop." Silas continues to laugh.

Grams has a bejeweled fist on each hip and she's staring spectral daggers at Silas. "It wasn't just vanity. I thought Jacob might come, and I was anxious to see my son."

I repeat her protest for his benefit, but it only makes him laugh all the harder.

"I don't think he believes you, Grams."

She crosses her arms and taps her noncorporeal foot in midair. "Well, I never."

Silas steeples his fingers and bounces his chin on the tips. "Why would you accept another gift from Mr. Bombay, especially after his previous treachery."

I'm not about to defend Rory, but we didn't actually prove "treachery" on that previous occasion, and he's done a bunch of nice stuff since. I swallow all of that, look down at the floor and mumble, "It was my birthday."

He stops in mid-jowl bounce. "Ah, so it was."

Grams darts between us like a pinball and exclaims, "What? Your birthday! Why wasn't I informed? Why didn't we have an enormous party?"

I pick at the seam of my jeans and swallow awkwardly. "It's no big deal. Birthdays weren't a thing when I was in the foster system, so I learned to lower my expectations. After a while, I kind of forgot about it. I had a big drunken bash for my twenty-first, but that was just an excuse for my friends to get trashed and embarrass me. I haven't had a real party since—since the year my mom died."

Grams slides her shimmering arm around my shoulders and does her best to give me a squeeze. "Well, I'm going to plan the biggest party this town has ever seen! A fancy-dress ball, with a live band, and—"

"Grams, you're dead. You can't organize a party. And if I have to do all the organizing, it will be like I'm planning some enormous narcissistic bash to feed my own ego. That feels more pathetic than no party. Let's just forget about it, all right?"

She pulls away and floats near my right shoulder. "That was a tad harsh, dear."

"Sorry. It's kind of a sore spot, you know?"

Little tears sparkle in the corners of her ethereal eyes. "How about a compromise?"

"I'm listening."

Silas chuckles. "Careful, Mitzy. It sounds like you're slipping into her web."

Grams ignores him and continues, "How about next year your father and I work together to plan the best twenty-third birthday any girl has ever had in all of history?"

I roll my eyes. "Way to start the negotiations high, Isadora."

Silas hides his grin behind a hand.

"How about you and dad plan a completely reasonable birthday party with only my closest friends? Let's say a maximum of ten guests. Deal?"

"Ten! Ten!" She clutches her pearls and flits around the room like a hummingbird on crack. "I can't possibly get the list below fifty."

I gasp and choke on my own laughter. "Fifty? I don't even know fifty people in this town, Grams. I will raise the limit to twenty-five guests. That's my final offer. Take it or leave it."

She zooms in, nose-to-nose. "I'll take it! But I

reserve the right to add five guests per year until you marry and give me at least one great grandchild."

My mouth hangs open like a broken cuckoo clock.

Silas leans toward me and places a comforting hand on my shoulder. "I don't want to hear her counter offer, but as your attorney, I'd advise you to take the deal. It will only get worse for you." He exhales in defeat.

I spit in my palm and extend my hand toward Grams. "Deal. You insane, delusional ghost!"

Grams grips my hand with surprising force and flashes her eyebrows. "Deal."

CHAPTER 9

THE BELL, BOOK & CANDLE is once again my happy home. I can see and hear Grams (whether I want to or not), interpret Pyewacket's variety of messages, and Silas is done being cross with me. I reach out to pick up the bracelet and make a closer inspection of the gift that stole my powers.

"Stop." My hand hovers above the bracelet and I glance at Silas.

"That was rude. You got it off my wrist. It's harmless now."

Silas lowers himself into the chair across the table and harrumphs into his mustache. "Is it?"

Oh brother. Whenever he starts a conversation in that tone of voice, I know there's a lesson right around the corner. "You utterly destroyed the clasp, so there's no way I can put it back on my wrist. It only works if it's complete, right?"

"Would you care to uncover a deeper truth?"

"How can I refuse such a cryptic offer, Silas?"

He shakes his head, obviously in no mood for snappy comebacks.

I fold my hands in my lap and sit up very straight. "Mr. Willoughby, would you please reveal the deeper truth to me."

Somewhere in the background I hear a ghost snicker, and my heart tingles with happiness.

"I believe your numerous gifts, clairvoyance, clairaudience, clairsentience, and claircognizance, can all be put to use in the field of forensics."

Squinting my eyes, I shake my head in confusion. "Forensics? Like a crime scene investigator? I'm not sure if I mentioned, but I dropped out of higher education. Sure, part of it was financial, but the rest was . . . let's say, an attention span issue."

He ignores my self-deprecation. "I believe this branch of forensics will provide the necessary quantity of intrigue."

I shrug. "All right, what books do I have to read?"

"Reading is a privilege, Mitzy. If I were to assign reading materials, you would feel fortunate to have the opportunity to explore such masterful tomes. However, this is a practical lesson. Reading will come later. Once your curiosity is piqued, you will be unable to resist the thirst for knowledge."

Silas highly underestimates my ability to resist things. My mother used to read to me every night before bed, and sometimes I would read to her. When she'd had a particularly hard day, or if she seemed more exhausted than usual, I would read to her until she fell asleep. In those months before the accident, it seemed like I was reading to her more and more. Once that horrible news knocked on my door, and my mother was taken from me forever, reading kind of lost its charm. I love books. I love this bookshop and all the promise it contains. I'm just not sure I can bring myself to crack a book without her. My chest feels tight and I can't swallow.

"Mizithra, you seem to have traveled to a place where I cannot follow."

I blink and take a deep breath. "Sorry, I just drifted off for a moment. I'm ready. What do I need to do?"

"You need to take control of your gifts, to take responsibility for your power. Rather than biding your time awaiting random messages, feelings, or images, with practice you can teach yourself to call this information at will. The forensics, at least with regard to the psychic realm, has much more to do with examining what has been, rather than interpreting what will be."

"I'm not super good with riddles, Silas."

"Indeed." He leans back and picks up a spoon from the counter. He places the spoon directly in front of me. "What can you tell me about the spoon?"

He can't be serious. "It's a spoon."

"Look deeper."

Reaching out with my left hand, I touch the spoon and feel the cold metal under my fingers. The sensation shifts to warm and I can smell coffee. I hear Twiggy's cackle echo through the labyrinth of my mind.

"Tell me what you have uncovered, Mitzy."

A slow grin spreads across my face. "Twiggy used this spoon to stir her coffee yesterday."

Silas steeples his fingers and places his chin on the tips. "Now the bracelet."

As I reach my left hand toward the bracelet, my fingers feel as though I'm slipping them into almost-set gelatin. I pull my hand back and rub my thumb and fingers together. They're dry. I reach toward the bracelet again. The closer my hand gets, the thicker the air becomes.

"What do you feel?"

"The air is different above the bracelet. It's—I don't know—thick?"

"Ah, yes. Thick is a good description. But you need to use all of your gifts to see this truth."

I place a finger on the bracelet and slide it toward me. I hear the word "trap," and I see a tiger in a cage. I touch the charm of Pyewacket, with the topaz eyes, and I feel power draining away. I feel empty and disconnected. As the messages fade, I forget what I was doing.

Silas reaches out with a firm hand and pulls the bracelet away from me.

Leaning back in my chair, I rub my forehead. "What happened?"

"The charm is powerful. Its effect was weakened when we destroyed the clasp and removed it from your wrist, but the charm lingers. And it seems to have been crafted specifically for you. Each time you impinge upon the bracelet, it resumes its effect on your powers. It will serve you well to recognize these subtle variations in your surroundings. To sense the harmful intention before it takes hold. Try again. Pay close and careful attention to the difference between the spoon and the bracelet."

The difference between a spoon and a bracelet? I mean, obviously one is jewelry and one isn't. And this is why I hated school. Pedantic, obvious lessons meant to waste time.

Placing my hand on the spoon, I feel nothing. I move my hand to the bracelet and feel a sharp prick on my finger. Yanking my hand back, I see a little drop of crimson red bubbling on the tip of my middle finger. I pop it in my mouth and attempt to complain, while I suck on the owie. "Um, that didn't happen before. What the heck is going on?"

Silas shakes his head. "I thought a tangible demonstration of the danger might be more fruitful."

"You did that? I don't think I want to learn any more about forensic magic."

"The study of matter and energy is far more than magic. And with your penchant for trouble, you would do well to pay closer attention to the true essence of the world around."

Before I can complain any further, the metal door from the alley slams home and the familiar stomp of Twiggy's biker boots brings a smile to my face.

"Hiya, Silas. What kind of trouble has the kid got herself into this time?"

Silas chuckles as he stands and offers his chair to Twiggy. "No more than usual. I'll be taking my leave. You ladies have a wonderful day." He places a hand on my shoulder and adds, "I hope you have learned your lesson about Mr. Bombay. Your grandmother and I have your best interests at heart, above all else." He slips the bracelet into a small black bag and places it in his pocket before he departs.

I nod, and a little piece of me itches for some Rory retribution.

Twiggy busies herself making coffee. "So that snake in the grass finally showed his true colors, eh, doll?"

"Yes. Everyone go ahead and have a good laugh at my expense. I was taken in by his lovely green eyes and his charming manners. Lesson learned. All right?"

Twiggy sets a cup of coffee in front of me and I'm so startled I can't speak.

"You take cream, right?"

I nod mutely.

She adds a little cream to my coffee and replaces the carton in the mini fridge.

"Seems like you're back early from your ski weekend, and that damaged bracelet on the table must have had its own story to tell."

I suddenly remember the SD card in my pocket. "It's a long and embarrassing story. But the highlights are: I tripped and fell onto a dead body at the ski resort, stole some keys off a maid's cart, searched the dead guy's room, and found this." I hold up the SD card.

Twiggy cackles so hard her face turns red and she pounds on her chest trying to catch her breath. "It just never gets old." She laughs a little longer.

Eager to change the subject, I ask, "Can you help me figure out the old computer so I can take a look at what's on here?"

"Nope."

"Twiggy, technically I'm your boss. Will you please turn on that computer and show me what's on this card?"

Nope."

Before I utter another sentence, I review the sequence of events. Twiggy has this thing about asking the right questions. So, I guess I'll try another approach. "*Why* won't you help me put this card in the computer and see what's on it?"

She smiles and nods. "I knew you'd figure it out. That old thing doesn't have an SD slot, and I've never had any use for a card reader here. I guess you'll hafta see if they carry 'em down at Rex's Drugstore, or maybe they can order one for you."

Of course, the town that tech forgot. "I don't have time to order something. I need to figure out someone who—" I stand up and slap my hand on the table.

Twiggy takes a step back.

"Quince Knudsen. He knows everything about photography. Even though he prefers using an old film camera, he must know how to get the info off this card." I pick up my mug of coffee and chug down several delicious gulps of java before I run upstairs to find a jacket and mittens.

Time to see if my breaking and exiting paid off.

CHAPTER 10

By the time I reach the *Pin Cherry Harbor Post* the interior of my Jeep hasn't even started to warm up. But I'm getting used to the daily implementation of survival techniques up north.

March, in Arizona, would've been T-shirt weather for sure. But today I'm wearing two layers of clothing under my warm coat plus a hat and gloves.

Parking directly across the street from the main entrance, I rush inside the old brick building, which houses the local paper. I instantly smell the ink. It always reminds me of my bookshop, but in a raw, straight-to-the-source kind of way. Approaching the birch-clad reception area, I ring the bell, which squats below a sign instructing me to do just that.

As usual, no one appears. They obviously aren't

closed on Sundays. The front door was unlocked. I ding the bell a few additional times and smile as Quince saunters around the corner looking sullen and unhappy at the interruption. However, when he sees me, his expression does shift.

"Hey, dude, what's up?"

Just to be clear, that's considered a verbose statement from this stoic high-school student, and I'm the "dude."

"Hey, Quince, I need some help."

A spark flickers in his dark eyes. "It'll cost ya."

I made the mistake of overpaying him on our first transaction several months ago, and despite our growing friendship he still views me as a handy ATM. "I'm happy to pay for your time."

He turns and walks into the back. I follow without an invitation, because I know there won't be one.

He walks toward the black cylindrical door that leads into his dark room, but I have to break the news to him. "Sorry, this is a modern tech situation."

He turns and his already curved shoulders sag another inch. He shuffles toward the single computer and plunks into the rolly office chair that is so old it's splitting at the seams. He extends a hand.

Like I said, he's a kid of few words. I place the SD card in his palm.

He looks up. “Where’d you get this?”

“It’s probably better if you don’t know.”

“I feel ya.” He pushes the card into a reader, already pigtailed to the machine.

“I’m surprised you have one of those. I thought you did all your photography on film.”

“My dad’s got a DSLR.”

I wait while Quince navigates to the card and opens a pane to reveal the contents.

“Can you just slideshow it?”

“Ya.” He clicks a few buttons, and the images flash by in sequence.

“It’s a bunch of pictures of fields?”

“Bad ones,” he mumbles.

I have to agree. There’s no composition, and no focal point. A few more bad landscape pictures scroll by followed by fence posts. “Wow, they get better.” I chuckle.

Quince grunts his agreement with a barely audible, “Snooze fest.”

Some of the fence posts have numbers stenciled directly on them and a few have metal signs affixed to them. “Hey, click on that one.”

He stops the slideshow and zooms in.

“Got any idea what that means?”

“Some kind of marker.”

I keep my snarky “keen grasp for the obvious” comment to myself and snap a photo with my phone. "Yup. Keep going."

He resumes the slideshow and we see several more marked fence posts, a few decent shots of the Fox Mountain Ski Resort, and the final image shows up with a "?" icon. "What does that mean? Why won't that display?"

"Not a JPEG."

This kid and Twiggy really know how to cut to the heart of things. "So what is it?"

"Probably an MOV."

As a film-school dropout, I'm quite familiar. "Can you play it?"

He nods and launches another program so he can play the digital movie.

"Is there sound?"

He taps a few keys, and we hear footsteps in the snow and breathing. Seems like those are the sounds of our intrepid filmmaker, but provide us no useful information.

The footsteps stop, and whoever is running the camera zooms way, way in. Now the shot frames two men standing in the shadow of an overhang at a building I don't recognize.

Quince mumbles, "Wide open, dude."

As though his words possess magical powers, the filmmaker must've had the same idea and opens up his aperture. The image immediately brightens, and the camera operator stealthily moves closer to the subjects.

Their voices are still faint, but now we can make out the image of the man facing the camera.

"Harold Doherty." Quince taps the image of the man's face.

"What? You recognize that guy?"

"Did a story last year. He's a big hotel developer from Chicago. Tried to buy Hawk Island from the tribe."

I'm momentarily dumbstruck by the sheer volume of words that Quince put forth. "Did he succeed?"

He chuckles. "Not even close."

"Can you up the volume?"

"It's not like on TV."

Point taken. Yet another movie trope fails to deliver. Turns out, if you didn't actually record decent sound, you can't manufacture it in post. "I hear you. Too bad this guy can't get a little closer." And once again, our words seem to direct the action.

The photographer creeps toward the two men. There's a crack, and I can only assume he's stepped on a fallen branch. The man with his back to the camera darts deeper into the shadows, while the guy Quince identified as Harold Doherty steps into the light and shouts, "Who's there?" He walks toward the cameraman.

Without even turning off his camera, the photographer runs and we can hear his feet crunching in the snow as his camera swings back and forth wildly. There's another loud crack, but this one sounds different.

"Gunshot," says Quince.

The cameraman falls and snow fills the lens.

Fade to black.

"Did we just witness a murder?" I put a hand over my mouth and shake my head.

"Doubt it."

"What makes you so sure? That was definitely a gunshot, and our guy went down."

He closes the file and turns to me. "No scream."

I pace behind his chair and replay the sequence mentally. Voices, branch, shouting, running, gunshot, falling. "You're right. No scream. But what makes you so sure he wasn't shot?"

"Have you ever been shot?"

I'm about to say no, when I remember my first day in Pin Cherry Harbor. "Actually, I have."

Quince turns and smiles with admiration. "Nice."

"It wasn't. It hurt like heck."

He laughs a little too hard. "Did you scream?"

"I get your point."

He closes the windows, clicks a few more buttons, and eventually ejects the card. As he hands it to me he repeats, "No scream."

"Thanks. But this Harold Doherty guy seems like a pretty good candidate for suspect number one."

"Pretty much."

I take the card, slip it in my pocket, and lay several twenties in the boy's hand. "You've got the solid makings of an investigative journalist."

He folds the bills and shoves them in his pocket, nods, and disappears through the rotating cylinder into his dark room.

And that's my clue that the conversation is over.

Next stop: City Hall.

I'll take the picture I snapped on my phone of those numbers on the fence posts and see if I can match it up with anything.

As I turn to leave, the hairs on the back of my neck tingle and the image of me busting out the window screen at Fox Mountain appears in my mood ring. That seems pretty clear. I can't take this SD card to the sheriff's station and tie myself directly to the incident in Oliver Kedrowski's room at the lodge. Maybe—

"Hey, do you have any way to get this SD card to the sheriff's station, anonymously?"

The black cylinder revolves to reveal Quince as he replies, "I'll handle it."

"But it'll cost me extra?"

"Correct." He grins.

I hand him the card and a few more bills.

First thing Monday morning, I drive to the central square in the historic district, which, if you ask me, describes the entire town.

Since Pin Cherry Harbor is also the county seat of Birch County, our city hall contains county records too. City Hall is picture perfect, almost like a scene from *To Kill A Mockingbird*. It stands about fifty feet tall. Three stories of solid granite with copper parapet walls. Inside I find terrazzo floors, ornamental plaster cornices, and marble walls at the elevator lobby. This must be the apple of Pin Cherry's eye—or more like the pin cherry. I chuckle to myself as I search the directory board for the clerk's office.

I'm not sure what I expected in the town that tech forgot, but when I show the clerk the photo on my phone, she points me to a chair and returns several minutes later with a small stack of folders.

"Those are public records, but they can't leave the building."

"All right, thanks."

I open the folders on the oak counter and page through the contents. There are a lot of detailed descriptions of what might be latitudes, longitudes, several mentions of various metes, and other things that could easily put a girl like me to sleep.

"Excuse me?" I give a friendly wave to the clerk.

She walks over with the speed of a box turtle on vacation.

I point to the notations on one of the maps. "Are these numbers GPS coordinates? Can I type the numbers into my phone to find the property?"

"Nope, not latitudes or longitudes. Those are bearings and distances. What you have here is a metes and bounds description. This type locates a point, gives bearing and distance to the next point, and so on all the way around and back to the point of beginning. Also known as the traverse."

I show her the picture on my phone once again. "Is this one of the points?"

She turns the phone, slips her bifocals from the top of her head to her nose, and peers at the image.

I wait, impatiently.

She turns the map toward her vantage point and runs her finger over the lines and numbers. She taps twice. "Right here. It's the benchmark."

I can almost hear Grams whispering her mantra about getting more flies with honey. "I'm sorry, but I'm quite new to all of this. What's a benchmark?"

"This one is the traverse."

I smile helplessly as I bite down on my own tongue.

Thankfully, she elaborates. "This is where you start. Then you walk the bearings and distances, per the map."

I feel compelled to tell her this is the crappiest map I've ever seen. But just as I'm winding up, she drops a juicy tidbit of information.

She points to a crisp white piece of paper in the folder. "See this? This indicates a survey's been completed within the last two weeks."

I stare at more meaningless numbers and measurements, but there is one line of interest. "What's this mean?"

"That note indicates the land that borders the surveyed area on two sides belongs to Fox Mountain Ski Resort."

Bingo! Now that's something I can sink my teeth into. "Can I get a copy of this page?" I hope that sounded innocent and not eager.

"Copies can be ordered on a Form 215." She points to a wall-rack filled with perfectly aligned forms. Six across and four deep. "The cost per page is $5.00 and orders take 7–10 business days."

Glancing around the utterly deserted room, I nod. Now she's stepping on my last nerve. "Excuse me, I've gotta take this call." I lift my phone to my ear and click the ringer to silent. "Yes, this is she . . ."

The clerk wanders away and I flip my camera phone on the survey order. CLICK. And the map. CLICK.

I wave as I walk toward the exit. "Thank you."

"Miss?"

Uh oh. "Yes?"

"Did you want to order that copy?"

When in doubt, lie it out. "I'll have to wait until I get paid on Friday. Thanks again."

She resumes reading her magazine and I skedaddle.

The reason the lie rolls so easily off my tongue is that I'd used it in truth many times before. I haven't forgotten where I came from. My humble, near-destitute history is never far from my mind.

CHAPTER 11

Armed with my super-spy photographs, surreptitiously taken at City Hall, and my knowledge of what was on Oliver Kedrowski's SD card, I drive back out to Fox Mountain. I'm beginning to think that Brandy's fears about some big hotel chain setting up competition are real.

The short road trip gives me the opportunity to rehearse several versions of the story I plan to tell Rory. Disappearing in the middle of the night and completely ghosting him for two days wasn't my finest moment.

I run through various scenarios involving legal matters with Silas, possibly my dad getting injured, or maybe Pyewacket being sick . . . But in the end, I'm too worried about the guilt I would suffer if one of my fabricated stories somehow came true simply to punish me.

It's probably best to make a vague reference to trouble at the shop and leave it at that.

The clouds have thickened and drawn closer to the earth. There's an icy fog rolling in from the partially frozen great lake and a frosty mist hangs in the air. I have to activate both my wipers and my fog lights.

Fog lights are yet another "new thing" that I've learned about since my arrival in Pin Cherry. I was under the impression that headlights covered all the bases. Silly me. I've since been told that there's some strange refractive property in fog that absolutely hates high beams and barely tolerates low beams. The solution is an ingenious pair of amber-tinted fog lights. Something about the lower intensity, and possibly even the color, cuts through the fog better than a brighter/whiter light. Who knew? Certainly not me.

When I pull into the parking lot in front of the main lodge, all of the wonder of my first visit has disappeared. Now I see the dilapidated building for what it truly is. A crumbling family heirloom propped up by history and legend. Water stains drip down the face of the building from the sharp-angled roof all the way to the first floor. The stains, peeling paint, and warped wooden trim seem so obvious today. The quaint, idyllic charm I once saw has vanished.

Inside, I approach the front desk. "Have you seen Brandy?"

The clerk at the desk looks up and squints her eyes. "I'm sorry, who?"

"Mrs. Hammer. The owner. Have you seen her?"

"Oh, I'm new. Her office is down that hallway." The woman gestures to the side hallway, where I stole the maid's keys. I'm not especially eager to retrace those steps. "I hate to disturb her. Would you mind calling her office?"

The receptionist openly rolls her eyes.

Part of me kind of admires the brazen move, while the heiress part of me is growing more and more offended by such crass behavior.

"Yes, Mrs. Hammer. She's here at the front desk. What? I don't know— Of course. One moment." The woman puts her hand over the phone and turns to me. "Name?"

"Mitzy Moon."

"It's Mitzy Moon. Of course. Yes, Mrs. Hammer." She hangs up the phone and stares at me with what I'd like to think is admiration. I can't be sure, but the disdain has definitely shifted. "She said to wait in the bar, Ms. Moon."

I smile and strut away with a little more self-importance than is absolutely necessary. But the moment I round the corner toward the main dining area and bar, my puffed up chest rapidly deflates.

"So, are you returning to the scene of the crime, Moon?"

"Excuse me?"

Deputy Paulsen's heavily-lidded eyes narrow and her right hand, as usual, rests on her gun. Her pudgy little fingers caress the handle, and I'm sure she's hoping for a reason to draw down.

"I am just here to meet—"

"Mitzy!"

A wave of relief washes over me as I hear Brandy's voice. "Hey, Brandy, I was hoping you'd have time for a quick cup of cocoa."

Brandy nods appreciatively. "For you? Always." She puts an arm around my shoulders and escorts me to the bar.

I sneak a peek over my shoulder at Deputy Paulsen and can barely contain my glee when I see the fury coloring her cheeks and the vein pulsing in her forehead. However, her comment about the scene of the crime has me a little concerned. File that under: Follow up later.

"How are you enjoying your stay on the mountain?" Brandy gives my shoulders a friendly squeeze.

It's weird that she's asking me about my stay,

as though I'm still staying here. Is it possible that she's completely unaware of my clandestine exit in the wee hours of Sunday morning? Let's hope. "I think you've done a wonderful job with the place." I keep my opinions about the general air of decomposition and the fondue-forward menu to myself.

She smiles, signals the bartender with her finger, and points to a booth in the corner. We slide onto the wooden benches, with the intricate tole painting along the ends, and I attempt to keep from getting tangled in the red-and-white checkered tablecloth.

She leans toward me and winks. "I can't tell you how nice it's been to have some girl talk. I'm so used to running this place, worrying about my daughter, and just putting out fires in general, I think I forgot how much fun a girl's night can be."

"I'm glad to hear it." I'm not quite sure how to get a handle on this conversation. My usual tactless lob from left field is definitely not the right approach. A sharp tingle on my left hand causes my eyes to dart to my mood ring. A sheriff's badge looms large in the swirling interior of the shiny cabochon.

"So, tell me about your bookshop." Brandy grabs her Sly Fox directly off the tray and the server miraculously manages to counterbalance the remaining mug and deliver it to me with only a minor slosh on the table.

"Thank you. That looks delicious." I wipe the spill with my napkin before anyone notices. Call it a severe case of "server empathy," but I feel for the guy. "The bookshop is wonderful. My grandmother had an amazing collection and I feel so fortunate that she left everything to me."

"You are lucky. At least your grandmother left you some cash." Brandy makes an exasperated gesture. "My ridiculous family just ran up the debts trying to keep this place afloat, and then dumped it in my lap. Maybe there'll be one more storm, a real big one. If I could get one more month out of the slopes, I might actually be able see the finish line."

"The skies definitely looked foreboding today. You might get your wish."

I catch the movement out of the corner of my eye right about the same time my clairsentience sends me a combination tummy tingle/chest crush. I turn. "Erick, would you like to join us?"

Brandy nods appreciatively at the approaching specimen. She whispers for my ears only, "Have you managed to crack that case?"

I chuckle and barely keep from spitting my boozy cocoa. "I wish."

Erick puts a hand on the table and nods to both of us. "Hello, ladies. What are you up to?"

I paint my face as the portrait of innocence and raise my mug. "Just some girl time."

Brandy clanks her mug to mine and adds, "Girls just wanna have fun."

We both take a big gulp of our yummy, warming beverages and share a giggle.

"Well, I'd hate to ruin your early start on the evening, but I need to borrow Miss Moon for just a minute."

Brandy winks at me and replies, "Of course, Sheriff. You borrow her as long as you want."

He blatantly ignores her implication and uses his most official voice. "Miss Moon, will you follow me?"

I slide obediently out of the booth and follow Erick. Struggling to keep my eyes from the danger zone, but the way that boy fills out a uniform . . . What's a girl to do?

He steps into the hallway, and yes it's *that* hallway, and shoves his hands in his pockets. "I hate to ask, but did you know the victim?"

I nearly spout Oliver's name out loud, but fortunately I remember that I shouldn't know that. "That body we found? You think I know that person?"

"I'm just trying to clarify a few things."

"Like what?" I'm powerless to control the fist that lands on my hip as I strike an obstinate pose.

"For starters, I'm a little curious how your fingerprints got in his room?"

Dear Lord baby Jesus! Why didn't I wear my gloves? "My fingerprints were in the victim's room? Please tell me you're not going to accuse me of murder, Erick."

"Not likely. But there is a chance that if the prints on the maid's key ring match a certain set of prints I have on file down at the station, I could be looking to charge you with breaking and entering." He crosses his strong arms over his chest in that delicious way that makes his biceps bulge, and I nearly lose my train of thought.

"I don't think you could call it 'breaking' if the key was used."

He rolls his eyes just a little and shakes his head as he exhales. "Moon, it'll go a long way toward keeping you out of trouble if you would just come clean with me. You and I both know you were in that room. If you can just give me a plausible explanation, I can probably see my way clear to make the breaking and entering go away."

I let my fist slip off of my hip and adopt a more cooperative stance. "How about I tell you what I know, and if I know something you don't know, then we forget all about this silly fingerprint business? Deal?"

Erick widens his stance before he replies. "That

would depend on what it is you think I don't know.
"

"Fair enough. Do you know the victim is Oliver Kedrowski?"

He nods. "We're waiting for confirmation from the ME, but that's our working theory."

I consider mentioning that Oliver worked for the *Tribune Times*, but I'm sure he's already discovered that too. I can't actually mention Harold Doherty or the suspicious video, since that will only incriminate me further. But maybe I can share the survey information. "Did you know that someone recently ordered a survey of the land abutting Fox Mountain?"

"What does that have to do with the victim?"

He's got me there. I call up the map on my phone and show him what parcel of land was surveyed. "I'm not sure it's connected. But the survey was just completed a couple of weeks ago and it seems like a strange coincidence."

He takes my phone and zooms in on the image.

Thankfully he hands the phone back to me without swiping left or right and uncovering my picture of Oliver's picture.

Erick rubs his hand over his full lips and comments, "The only thing that's interesting about that survey is that it's for Legacy Land."

Raising one eyebrow I ask, "For what now?"

"The Natural Resources Department runs a land conservation program. They look for pristine forest that owners are willing to permanently protect, and then the parcel is placed in the state's Legacy Land program."

I shrug. "Why?"

He tilts his chin down and gives me a half-smile. "Because protected wildlands are disappearing. Because big hotel chains and big-box stores are buying up land and destroying habitat faster than you can say abracadabra, I guess."

As soon as Erick says "big hotel chains" the hairs on the back of my neck stand up and tingle so hard I nearly jump out of my own skin. Now I understand why Oliver was taking all those pictures. They had something to do with the land survey and with Harold Doherty. How can I work that into a conversation? "Well, if a survey was ordered, doesn't that mean someone is interested in the land?"

"Possibly. There are a variety of reasons for a survey. The property adjacent to Fox Mountain has been part of the Legacy Land program for decades. I can't imagine why they'd be ordering a survey now."

"Maybe the owners wanted to take it out of the legacy program."

"Impossible. That's the whole purpose of the

program. Once the land goes in, it's protected in perpetuity."

"Copy that. Is that enough information to get me off the hook?"

Erick uncrosses his arms and sighs in defeat. "I have to admit, Moon, you're probably of more use to me on the outside. I'll break the bad news to Deputy Paulsen."

"What bad news?"

"The news that she won't be arresting you today."

My jaw drops and I stare in genuine shock. "Arresting me?"

"Despite your innocent face, your prints were in the room, and your prints were on the key ring I found in the snowbank outside the victims window. It's more than enough to place you in room 237. And if I know you, you didn't leave empty-handed."

I swallow and widen my eyes with innocence. "You know my rule, if I find anything useful I'm always willing to share."

"Oh, I remember the rule. It just seems that the timeline of when the useful intel gets shared is a little fuzzy."

Digging into my very small bag of tricks, I lean close to Erick and whisper, "What's wrong with a few blurred lines, Sheriff?"

He blushes adorably and stammers unintelligibly.

Without waiting for his reply, I casually inhale a whiff of his woodsy-citrus scent and hustle back to the booth to make my excuses with Brandy.

"Sorry. That didn't go well, as you might've expected. I need to take care of a couple things."

She's on her second or third mug of spirited cocoa and seems unflappable. "Don't worry about it. You do you, sweetie. Come find me later if you need s'more girl power." She raises her cup.

I toss out a fake laugh and make my escape before she secures any definitive promise.

Time for Rory Bombay to pay the piper. And, to be clear, I'm the piper.

CHAPTER 12

SINCE EVERYONE SEEMS to believe I'm still staying at the hotel, I'm wondering if Rory has remained in his room?

I hurry out of the elevator and across the faded carpet lying listlessly in the hall. As I approach the door to his accommodations, my nerve starts to wither. I pace and chew the inside of my cheek.

Before I can make up my mind, the phone in his room rings out at that classic 100-decibel, hotels-only volume. I step to the side to make sure the shadow of my feet isn't visible under the door, and press my ear to the thin wall.

"Hello. Mr. Bombay speaking. Oh, hi— Why wouldn't you want me to say your name? I see. Thank you for letting me know."

Thank heaven for shoddy construction.

I tiptoe back toward the elevator and push the button. Once that classic "BONG" echoes down the hallway, I stomp toward Rory's room and knock loudly. Hopefully my ruse is convincing and he'll never suspect I overheard the call.

The door opens and Rory smiles pleasantly. However, now that my powers have been un-chained, or rather un-charmed, I sense the mixture of fear and loathing skulking just beneath the surface.

"Won't you come in?" He makes a grand ges-ture and steps back.

"Of course."

As the spring on the door creaks and slams the portal shut with more force than necessary, I imme-diately regret my decision. Retribution can wait. How about a plan to get the heck out of here? "Have you eaten? Do you want to grab an early dinner?"

Rory takes a seat on the whitewashed wooden chair next to the tiny built-in desk and shakes his head. "I had a late lunch—alone."

Wow, he's not wasting any time heaping on the guilt. "Sorry about that. I just got back and came to offer an explanation."

He crosses his arms and leans back. "I'm listening."

"I couldn't sleep the other night, and my naturally snoopy nature got me into a little bit of trouble. I kind of had to 'flee the scene' until the coast was clear." That sounded way more *Butch Cassidy and the Sundance Kid* than I intended.

His arms uncross and he straightens himself in the chair. "You left alone? All by yourself?"

"Just me and the shuttle driver." I laugh and shrug helplessly.

He exhales, and I sense a distinct shift in his energy. He's not exactly pleased, but there's a tinge of anticipation in the air that definitely wasn't there a moment ago.

"So, again, sorry to disappear." Here's hoping that my lame excuse was both informative enough and vague enough to keep me in his good graces.

"You could've called, or texted."

Not sure why he said texted with such disdain, but I keep forgetting how old-fashioned he is. If Silas and my grandmother's stories can be believed, they had a nasty run in with Mr. Rory Bombay almost fifteen years ago. Theoretically, he would've been more than fifteen at that time and that means he's . . . Who knows? I wasn't there and I'm no fan of math. "How about I make it up to you and buy you a drink at the bar?"

He looks away. "I'm thinking of giving it up for Lent."

My eyes widen and I open my mouth to retort but—

"Gotcha." He chuckles. "Why don't I order a bottle of champagne for the room."

I dislike where this is headed, but since I'm about to confront him with some seriously heavy accusations, he's probably better off with a glass or two of champagne in him. "Sure."

He walks to the telephone next to the bed and calls room service. I take the opportunity to seat-jack him and occupy the one and only chair in the room. It's definitely a commentary on the lack of sophistication at Fox Mountain, if Rory Bombay is in a room this sparsely appointed.

Rory hangs up the phone, turns, and smirks. He sits on the bed and we wait.

"Take off your coat and stay a while, Miss Moon."

I laugh, unzip my coat, and wriggle out of it. As soon as I'm free of the parka, I see his eyes dart to my left wrist. Great. Looks like we'll be having the conversation without the benefit of alcohol.

"You've removed your bracelet. Did you not like it?"

Despite his annoyingly worded question, I think my only option here is to go in guns blazing. "Where did you get that bracelet?"

His face is a mask of mock surprise. "That's a

rather uncouth question! Gifts are to be enjoyed, not investigated."

"It's a little hard for me to enjoy a gift that was meant to put me in a cage."

His emerald-green eyes shift to a dark, brooding forest green and I hear his teeth grind together.

"Don't bother denying it this time. You knew exactly what you were giving me. What I want to know is, why?"

Without warning, there is a strange electricity in the air, and my mood ring burns on my finger. I don't dare risk a glance. Instead, I use the forensic magic techniques that Silas is teaching me. And I sense some manipulation of energy coming from Rory.

There's no way I'm gonna allow him to control me—ever again. I grab my coat and bolt for the door.

He stands. "Mitzy, where are you going?"

"I left my phone in the bar. I need to grab it."

"Are you coming back?"

It's a fair question, after I ran out in the middle of the night without telling him. "I'll tell you what. When you're ready to be honest with me, completely honest, we'll get together." I hurry out the door and run directly into room service.

Stemware goes flying. CRASH!

The champagne bottle hits the floor. BOOM!

And Mitzy Moon lands on her well-padded backside.

Glass and champagne foam coat everything, including me.

"I'm so sorry, Miss—"

"It was totally my fault." I jump up, shake off as much glass as I can, and sprint for the elevator, sliding in *Risky Business* style just before the doors close.

Once inside the relative safety of the lift, I brush off the rest of the glass, shake the champagne off my coat, and prepare to pump some information from Brandy. She should be liquored-up enough to let something useful slip. Maybe she even knows Harold Doherty and can finger him for the murder.

Back in our cozy booth, I've lost track of Brandy's drink count. This girl can really put them away. I attempt to get the "sharing" ball rolling by telling her about my bad luck with men.

She's surprisingly eager to jump on that topic.

"Men! Can't live with 'em, can't kill him." She lifts her latest martini. "I'll drink to that."

I lift my glass and move it to my lips, but set it down without actually drinking. It's an old trick from my days in poverty. Make one drink last all night; no one's the wiser. Of course, on those fortunate evenings when some overeager frat boy was buying the drinks, I could put them away as easily as my current booth-mate.

"What about you, Brandy? Have you got anyone on the hook?"

She drains her martini, wipes her mouth with the back of her hand, and spits on the table.

That's new. "Wow, he must've done you wrong."

"I was really good to him, you know. I comp'd his room, his meals. I even skied his pass."

Attempting to interpret drunken Brandy-speak, I ask, "You gave him a ski pass?"

She nods vigorously and then grabs her head.

I subtly signal the waiter to keep his distance.

He nods and rolls his eyes.

"So this guy didn't appreciate your generosity?"

"Generosity." She slams her hand down on the table, narrowly missing the martini glass. "He just used me. You know. He used me." She looks as though she might cry.

"Well, that sucks. Did you kick him out, at least? Of the lodge, I mean?"

She laughs maniacally. "Oh, it's so much better." More wild laughter.

The hairs on the back of my neck tingle. "What did you do?"

"I shouldn't tell you. I shouldn't tell anyone."

"It's just us girls. You can tell me."

She leans forward and gestures with her left hand, knocking the martini glass over, but not breaking it.

I move it to the end of the table and slide my own glass out of the danger zone. "Brandy? What did you do?"

"I wen' and got a love potion. It was guaranteed. So he'd 'solutely love me forever."

The hairs on the back of my neck are dancing the tango, and my mood ring is alternating hot and cold flashes. "A love potion? Where would you get something like that?"

"I shouldn't say. I'm not s'pose to say."

I decide to stick with tried and true at this point. "It's just us girls. You can tell me."

She leans even closer, and her breath could start a forest fire. "It was from a real live tipsy."

Oh, someone's tipsy all right. "Do you mean gypsy?"

"Yeah." Brandy makes a motion with her hand to indicate a crystal ball. "A gypsy!"

Suspicion confirmed. It's got to be one of my grandmother's old archrivals, Ania Karina Nowak. She runs a palm-reading, tarot, and, apparently, potion shop on the outskirts of Pin Cherry Harbor.

"It was guar—gor—gra, promised it would work. Cost me an arm and a leg. Maxed out my last credit card." Brandy slams her fist on the table and angry tears spill from her eyes. “Lying gypsy rich.”

Okey dokey. Time for me to get Mrs. Hammer out of the bar. We’re definitely attracting the wrong kind of attention. “Hey, Brandy, can I take you to your apartment?”

Her glassy eyes struggle to focus on my face and she slurs her words. “You wanna come over? You wanna hangout?”

What I’d like to do is find out if someone is actually watching her daughter, and get Brandy out of this very public area before irreversible damage is done. “I’d love to hang out. Let me help you up.”

She grabs onto me like a drowning swimmer on a lifeguard and continues to slur her words together. “You’re agoodperson. You’re mybestfriend.”

If I had a dollar for every time I’d uttered that drunken phrase in my misspent youth . . . “That’s it. Just lean on me and tell me which floor to take us to.”

“It’s not here. It’s out there.”

Great, now I have to wander around in the freezing cold with the drunken version of Siri for my GPS. I steer Brandy toward the front desk, but before I make it to my destination, the bartender sidles up behind me and whispers, “There’s a gator out front. Turn left at the end of the sidewalk, follow the signs to the Vixen’s Lair.”

I turn and shake my head.

He shrugs. "She named it."

I half carry/half drag Brandy out to the waiting vehicle, a cross between a miniature truck and a golf cart, apparently called a gator, and start it up. The signs are evenly spaced and well lit, which leads me to believe I'm not the first person to take a drunk Mrs. Hammer back to her abode. I knock, and a deadbolt slowly scrapes against its metal housing before a small bent woman inches open the front door. The weight of the warped wooden planks seems to get the better of her and she stops abruptly when she sees me staring at her.

"Her room is straight in the back."

No introduction. No questions.

I walk straight to the back and lay Brandy on her bed. I slip off her boots and cover her with a blanket.

It's the kind of thing no one ever did for me, but I wish they would've. There's no sign of the daughter, but clearly the elderly woman isn't here for Brandy's sake.

I quietly make my way back toward the open front door.

The miniscule old woman steps out of the shadow of the kitchen.

I stop and attempt a reassuring smile.

She seems surprised that I've taken the time to acknowledge her efforts. "Thank you, dear."

"You're welcome. Are you Brandy's mother?"

"Yes, I am."

I'm not exactly sure what to say to a woman who's trying to hold her family together and, not by choice but by necessity, has been relegated to nanny. Without even asking, I'm sure it's her love for her granddaughter that keeps her in this little cottage night after night. There just aren't any words. I open my arms and offer the woman a warm hug.

She leans toward me and takes a ragged breath.

Her body is frail and almost weightless, but the hug reminds me so much of my own grandmother that emotions bubble up and I have to blink back my own tears before hurrying into the frosty night air.

Leaving the gator parked in front of Brandy's cabin, I run through the packed snow, up to the hotel parking lot to find my Jeep.

The winding road leaving Fox Mountain is pitch black before moonrise. Despite my improved winter driving skills, I take it slow on my return trip to Pin Cherry Harbor. The last thing I need to do is hit a moose on this deserted road and die of hypothermia waiting to be discovered.

But the deep darkness reminds me of Arizona

and the strange, stunted life I left behind. How many times have I been the "Brandy?" I shudder to think. In fact, I struggle to remember a single thing about my life that was better before I hopped on that malodorous bus and headed north.

One thing is for sure, first thing in the morning, Silas Willoughby is going to hear all about this gypsy love potion.

CHAPTER 13

SILAS AGREES to meet me at the patisserie on Third Avenue for breakfast. He's concerned that Odell may be beginning to suspect I've inherited my grandmother's gift for visions, and Silas has yet to develop a plausible cover story.

No doubt Odell would be shocked to learn that, not only did I inherit my grandmother's clairvoyance, but also, somehow, I have a full set of psychic gifts.

Unable to face the deathly cold wind knifing across the lake, I opt to drive to Bless Choux.

I park across the street and have a good laugh when I see Silas's 1908 Model T. How he drives that in the winter, I will never know. But I suppose people drove it in the winter back in the 1900s. It's not like weather is a new invention.

Hurrying across the street, I open the door to the bakery and inhale deeply. Ah, why does pastry smell so heavenly?

Silas nods his bald head in my direction and I slip onto the seat opposite him.

"I took the liberty of ordering you a hot chocolate and one of those chocolate croissants you're so fond of."

"Thanks. You know me too well."

Anne stops at the table, sets down her tray, and unloads the contents. "Good morning Mitzy, how do you like the spring weather?"

I look up, and, if not for the added benefit of my extrasensory perceptions, I wouldn't be able to tell whether she's serious. My clairsentience confirms she actually feels this is lovely spring weather. "It's a little chilly for an Arizona girl, but I hear the locals are happy."

"Indeed, at this rate we'll be putting our lawn chairs in the snowbank and getting a decent tan before the end of April!" She scoops up her tray, nods, and giggles all the way back to the kitchen.

I look at Silas and shake my head. "I think it's freezing, and I think she might be crazy."

Silas chuckles until his cheeks turn red and his jowls shake. "Anne never fails to see the sunny side of life. I think that's what everyone appreciates about her."

Taking a careful sip of my steaming cocoa, I utter an audible “yum” as the cinnamon-kissed chocolate trickles down my throat and warms my belly. “Oh boy, do I have some news for you.”

“By all means, proceed.” Silas carefully stirs the whipped cream into his hot chocolate to avoid decorating his mustache, and dives into his croissant with a knife and fork while I regale him with my news.

“What would you say if I told you that Brandy Hammer, the owner of Fox Mountain, obtained a love potion from—”

“That infernal gypsy woman.” The disdain in Silas’s voice is palpable.

“Wow! Why don’t you tell me how you really feel?”

Silas fixes me with an odd look. “I believe I did.”

I shake my head. “It’s an expression. Let’s not get lost in it. Is there any way for me to trace a potion? Like the way you’re teaching me to recognize charmed objects, could I recognize someone under the influence of a potion?”

“I doubt that gypsy has the skill to create a legitimate potion. I fear she has found yet another way to bilk her customers with nothing more than snake oil.”

“Snake oil? Like venomous?”

Silas chuckles. "I believe it's what you would call an *expression*. Clearly a reference from before your time."

I purse my lips and raise an eyebrow. "Do you think I should let Erick know?"

Silas carefully sets down his knife and fork and wipes his mouth with the corner of his napkin. "To what end?"

"I don't know. But she shouldn't be selling fake crap to people should she? I mean, it's kind of sheisty."

Silas shrugs. "Perhaps it is none of your concern. However, if you truly wish to pick up Isadora's mantle, then your information may be of some interest to the sheriff."

The implication that I would pick up my grandmother's feud and carry it out for another generation is offensive and heartwarming at the same time. I don't want to be known as petty, but the idea that I have a family feud all my own like the Hatfields and McCoys . . . It gives me a happy heart. "Maybe I will continue the feud. I'm not sure unscrupulous gypsies should be allowed to operate freely."

"Fair enough. It would appear that you have managed to manufacture a legitimate justification for paying a visit to Sheriff Harper." Silas winks and dives back into his croissant.

It's my turn to chuckle. "Advantage, Willoughby."

He snickers at my tennis reference as he thoughtfully chews.

I order a slice of quiche to back up my croissant consumption and enjoy every wonderfully warm, fluffy bite of my bacon and Swiss delight. "I think I'll walk over to the station. That's a lot of buttery, flaky pastry crust sitting heavy in my tummy."

Silas nods. "You'll update me, of course?"

"Of course. By the way, any leads on *Saducismus Triumphatus*?"

He shakes his head mournfully. "A great loss. Breaks my heart. It was the first volume Isadora acquired for the Rare Books Loft. Not only have we lost a piece of arcane history, but I fear we've lost a little piece of Myrtle Isadora's history as well."

This news weighs heavy on my heart. Family, and the nostalgia that accompanies it, has gained a great deal of importance to me in the last few months. "Should I file a report when I'm at the station?"

Silas glances up at me. "Yes, that would be prudent. A police report will be required for the insurance claim."

"Insurance claim?"

"Twiggy has no doubt informed you of the value of your rare books collection. I would be remiss if I had not instructed your grandmother to insure such a valuable asset."

"Copy that. I'll file a report and update you later."

I wave to Anne and rub my tummy with delight as I leave.

She chuckles and resumes assisting her customers.

The spring sun is gaining strength and the temperature has actually climbed high enough that the steady pitter-patter of melting snow and ice offers a strange accompaniment on my walk to the sheriff's station on Main Street.

Stepping inside, I stomp off my boots on the dingy floor mat and proceed to the counter.

Furious Monkeys sits at the desk, busily tapping and swiping on her phone. Almost certainly playing the addictive game for which I've nicknamed her, but it shocks me motionless when she looks up. "Hey, Mitzy. Been kidnapped lately?" She laughs at her own joke and returns to her game.

Deputy Baird (her actual name) may or may not have been part of the team which rescued me from one of my misadventures, but that's another story entirely.

There's only one officer in the sheriff's station-that-time-forgot. He sits at his dented metal desk, hand writing a report. He looks up as I pass, but I quickly shift my gaze to the terribly interesting wood paneling behind him.

No sign of Deputy Paulsen, which is always a plus.

I peek into Erick's office, but he's on the phone. So, I wait outside like a polite adult.

"Well, that doesn't make any sense. We can't find out where it came from if we don't know what it is. Double check your results and get back to me." He bangs down the receiver with what I feel is an unnecessary amount of force, exhales, and leans back in his chair. "Come on in, Moon."

I don't care for his tone, but at least we've dropped "Miss" from the moniker. "Bad news?"

He laces his fingers behind his head, and as usual my eyes wander and lap up every pixel of the lovely image before me.

He ignores my question. "What brings you in?"

Taking a seat that wasn't offered, I politely respond to his question even though he overlooked mine. "A couple of things. I need to file a report for a theft at the bookshop, and I came across a strange piece of information that may or may not prove useful."

"Speaking of which, you wouldn't happen to know anything about an SD card that was pushed through the mail slot in the front door of the station by someone wearing a ski mask and gloves, would you?"

Internally I'm thrilled with Quince's flair for the dramatic, but externally I school my features once again into a portrait of innocence. "An SD card? I don't even have a camera."

Erick chuckles and leans forward. "Why does that answer not surprise me?"

I adjust the collar of my jacket and shrug.

"So this theft at the bookshop. Another break-in?" he asks.

"I don't think so. The new security system is solid. I think this jerk actually stole the book during that fundraiser we had last week."

"A book? You want to file a police report on a missing book? I'm not sure if that would even qualify as a petty crime." Erick smiles as he rubs the back of his neck with one hand.

"It's not just any book. It's like three hundred years old, and it's insured and everything, according to Silas."

He tilts his head in a way that indicates I've piqued his interest. "Your place was crawling with people that night. No one saw the theft?"

"We were hosting a fundraiser for the animal shelter. It's not like we had security on site—" As soon as I utter the words, I realize my terrible mistake.

Erick leans back and I see the momentary hurt in his eyes. "Actually, I think you did have security."

"Sorry. Well, did you see anything suspicious?"

He laughs off the uncomfortable situation. "Twiggy called me down to walk Amaryllis to her car with the cashbox, but other than that I never left the loft."

"I guess I'll talk to my dad and Amaryllis to see if they have a copy of the guest list."

"It's a good place to start. What's the other information you have for me?"

"I was out at Fox Mountain—"

"I'm aware." His bright blue eyes turn stormy and he crosses his arms as he glares.

A toddler having a snit would be subtler. Clearly Erick hasn't forgiven me for my ski date. I'd love to tell him that I dropped Rory like a hot, rotten potato, but it's really none of his business. "Anyhow, I got to know the owner, Brandy Hammer. We were having drinks last night."

Erick shakes his head. "I hate to break it to you, but Brandy's not real discerning about who she has drinks with."

"I figured that out pretty quick. The point is, after she'd had a few, she told me that she'd recently picked up a love potion from a gypsy."

"For herself?"

"No way. She gave this love potion to her

boyfriend, or at least some guy she wanted to be her boyfriend."

"Name?"

"No. But she did mention that she'd given him a free room, meals, and a ski pass. There should be some record of that."

"Why is this any of my concern?"

"I don't know. It just seems like a shady thing to be selling people. And it's my understanding that this gypsy woman has had some less than legitimate business transactions in the past."

Erick leans back and his chair creaks as he laughs. "Oh, that's your understanding, is it? Did someone bring you up to speed on your grandmother's history with Mrs. Nowak?"

"In fact, someone did." I'll go ahead and let him assume it was Silas, which is partially true. The fact that my grandmother chimed in with her side of the story is none of his concern. "Can I file that stolen book report with you?" I give him my best attempt at a sexy smile.

He bursts into what can best be described as the giggles.

"Rude."

He catches his breath, wipes a little laughter-tear from the corner of his eye, and explains. "It was just the way you put the emPHAsis on the wrong syllABle." He chuckles a little bit more.

"I can appreciate that reference, Erick. *View from the Top*? The circa 2003 Mike Myers movie?"

He nods and continues in a calmer tone. "You said 'file the stolen book report,' which obviously makes it sound like you stole a book report from a poor little elementary school kid. I don't know, jokes aren't funny when you have to explain them."

I give him a courtesy chuckle. "Copy that. So about that report?"

He presses a button on his phone, "Deputy Baird, I need you to take a stolen property report for Miss Moon. I'll send her to your desk."

Walking toward the door, I look over my shoulder demurely. "Thanks, Erick."

He shakes his head. "Still Sheriff Harper."

I add a scandalous wink. "If you insist."

"I always do, for all the good it does." He smiles warmly at me, and those beautiful blue eyes light up for just a moment.

That smile will get me through three days, at least. "Thanks." I walk out of Erick's office and Deputy Baird waves me toward her desk. I file my report and head back to the bookshop to fill in Grams on all the big doings.

CHAPTER 14

Back at the Batcave, Silas is patiently waiting for me while Grams writes him notes, and Pye sits atop a bookshelf studying Mr. Willoughby's bald head.

Pyewacket takes one look at me, leaps down from the shelf, and retrieves a plush frog puppet from the children's book area.

I accept the gift that's laid at my feet. "Do you wanna play?" I slip my hand inside the puppet and attempt to "attack" Pye.

He turns, lifts his tail haughtily, and saunters away without a backward glance.

"I'll take that as a 'no,' you spoiled brat." I toss the puppet back from whence it came.

"Poor Mr. Cuddlekins," Grams coos after the entitled feline.

Silas clears his throat and asks, "Were you successful in filing the stolen property report?"

"Yes, sir. But I didn't tell him about the Harold Doherty connection."

"Indeed. Wouldn't want to incriminate yourself." His jowls wag and he bobs his head.

"I did mention the love potion, but Erick didn't seem to take that too seriously."

Grams whips into the middle of our conversation and wags her finger in my face. "That dishonest gypsy woman is up to no good. If this town would wake up and smell the iron ore, they'd realize she's been stealing from them for decades!"

"Easy, Leona Helmsley, Silas and I are on your side."

Silas nods confirmation and gestures to Isadora. "Is she upset about the gypsy woman?"

"Was that an excellent guess, or do you have some psychic powers of your own?" I chuckle.

He frowns. "It was an educated deduction."

"Did you get the ME's report?"

He does not respond.

I exhale and make another attempt. "May I see the report, please?"

Silas gives my afterthought manners a perfunctory nod. "Certainly." He hands me the pages.

I trace my finger over the report, looking at time

of death, identity of the victim, and finally cause of death.

"Poison? I thought he was shot?"

"What led you to that hypothesis?"

"I could've sworn I saw blood in the snow around the body."

He strokes his mustache with a thumb and first finger. "*Sanguinaria canadensis.*"

I look at Grams and raise my hands in a "no idea" gesture.

She shakes her head and shrugs her designer-gown-clad shoulders.

"Is that supposed to mean something to me, Silas?"

Silas paces as he replies. "The common name is bloodroot. In this area, some consider it a harbinger of spring. Most likely what you observed was the flower's life leaking onto the snow. Stems, leaves, and even roots will 'bleed' when they are broken or damaged. Perhaps the killer disturbed a small stand of bloodroot when they discarded the body."

"Dumped the body? You don't think he was killed there?"

"I would find it highly unlikely that a man would wander into the woods, ingest a poison, and lie down to await death." Silas tamps down his mustache to punctuate his opinion.

"Maybe he didn't know he'd taken the poison."

"Perhaps, but if this poison ultimately caused the cardiac failure noted in the report, it would stand to reason that there were symptoms preceding death. I still find it burdensome to believe that an individual under the influence of such a powerful toxin would see fit to go for an excursion.

"He was a photojournalist, and he was investigating something shady. Maybe he was meeting with an informant."

Silas nods, but then shakes his head. "And you propose this informant turned into a murderer?"

"No idea. For now let's just stick with what we know. The victim was Oliver Kedrowski, a photojournalist for the *Tribune Times*. He was poisoned, which definitely points to murder, and his room—"

Grams zooms down in front of my face. "What is it? Are you having a vision?"

I blink and swallow. "I don't think it's psychic. I just put two and two together. Brandy told me she gave her boyfriend a free room, and I heard her yelling at the maid not to let anyone into room 237. Maybe Oliver Kedrowski was the boyfriend."

Grams swirls around me. "That does make sense. Maybe she was pressuring him to take bigger risks to get more information about the people surveying the land adjacent to the ski resort."

"Right. And she would've wanted the potion to

make sure he would stay loyal to her and be so smitten he'd do anything she asked."

Silas walks over and places a hand on my shoulder. "I'm only receiving half of this conversation, Mitzy. However, it sounds to me as though Mrs. Hammer could potentially be our poisoner."

"Maybe, but it doesn't make total sense. She wouldn't have wanted to kill Oliver. She wanted him to break the story, and prevent competition from setting up anywhere near her resort."

"You're making several assumptions."

"Like what?"

"Preeminently, you are assuming that whoever surveyed the adjacent land did so for the purpose of establishing a competitive business."

"Is that really such a huge leap?"

"Perhaps not. Continue."

"I don't think she would have killed Oliver. She seemed really broken up about her boyfriend disappearing. Maybe he was allergic to something in the love potion and there was an unexpected reaction."

"And how do you propose to explain her deception?"

"What deception?"

"The report states ingestion of unidentified toxin as the initial cause in the chain of events that ended with cardiac arrest. She failed to call the police."

I spin around and throw my hands in the air. "All right, you have a point. If she gave the potion to Oliver and he had a bad reaction, her first instinct should've been to call paramedics. If she loved him, why didn't she try to save him?"

"That's a good question, dear. I think you'd better get back out to Fox Mountain and talk to this Brandy Hammer."

Translating for Silas, I share Ghost-ma's suggestion. "Grams thinks I should head back out to the mountain and find out why Brandy didn't call the paramedics."

"And what if you run into Mr. Bombay?"

"Why would he still be at the resort?"

Silas does not answer my question, but instead raises a new idea. "Perhaps it is time for you to take a more active approach to your gifts."

"I learned the energy sensing thing, and I figured out when Rory was trying to manipulate me. I got myself out of the room. I'm fine."

"The best defense is a good offense."

"Sorry, Silas, I never really played sports. I more or less hung with a crowd that skipped school and got into trouble."

Grams enjoys a lovely chuckle at my expense.

"Why does that not surprise me?" Silas harrumphs. "What I'm suggesting, Mizithra, is that you learn to perform a transmutation. Rather than waiting for Rory to take some action against you, I suggest you protect yourself by disabling his greatest weapon."

"His greatest weapon? Which is?" I scrunch up my nose as I search my mental archives.

"Manipulation of perception."

I don't like the sound of that at all, and I like the implication even less. "Are you saying Rory has some kind of mind control?"

"Exactly. My assumption is that he subtly warps reality in a way that forces people to see only the best of him. Perhaps he even pushes them to believe things that are less than authentic. Subconsciously pushing them to take his side, or trust him implicitly."

I rub my naked left wrist and my cheeks color with embarrassment. "He did use the charm bracelet to block my ability to connect with my psychic gifts and sense what he was actually up to."

"The charm bracelet robbed you of your greatest protections. That was no simple manipulation, Mitzy. Whether you are ready to believe it or not, I fear there was true malice behind his present."

"I'm still a little on the fence, but you're not wrong. What do you want me to learn?"

"I feel it would behoove you to identify the veil

of falsehood and learn to remove it and expose the truth which lies beneath."

"In English, please."

Grams floats in to my rescue. "He wants to teach you the truth symbols. He wants you to learn how to prevent someone from lying."

I raise an eyebrow. "Truth symbols? That does sound useful."

Silas shakes his head vigorously and his jowls waggle to and fro. "This is no parlor trick. This is a powerful transmutation, and you should know better than most how truth can be a double-edged sword. It is not a skill to be abused. It is a potent tool, to be wielded with the precision of a scalpel."

"All right. All right. What must I do?"

Silas leads the way up the circular staircase to the Rare Books Loft and procures a small book, sheathed in blood-red leather, from the bottom shelf of one of the bookcases. He lays the volume on an oak reading table and pulls the chain dangling below the green-glass lampshade. A bright light illuminates the pages and the scent of history wafts toward me as he carefully leafs through the contents. Eventually he stops and motions for me to join him next to the table. "These symbols have many meanings. Putting them together in the precise order, which I will teach you, is the key to lifting the veil." He straightens and looks at me. "Not the veil between the worlds, the veil between truth and falsehood."

The film student in me wants ominous but hopeful music to swell; the girl standing in the middle of her own bookshop gets no such soundtrack. "I'm ready."

Silas tilts his head and a warm light sparks in his milky-blue eyes. "Yes, I believe you are."

He shows me the first symbol.

I trace the symbol with my finger. "Easy enough. What's next?"

His spine straightens in that alchemical-wizardy way that I always find unsettling. "This is not a game, Mizithra. These are not a child's doodles to be toyed with and tossed aside. Symbols have power. That power can only be accessed through focused intentionality. Not your halfhearted and flippant forays."

While most of me feels adequately scolded, the teeny part of me that relies on humor to create a protective shell finds itself unable to resist laughing at the alliteration. "I totally understand. I will definitely work more on focus and less on flippant forays."

Now Grams giggles.

"Grams! You're not helping!"

Silas removes his magicked spectacles from the inner pocket of his tattered tweed coat, slips them on, and scowls at Grams. "Isadora, I must ask you to leave us. This lesson is of no use to you and your distractions are unwelcome."

Grams opens her mouth to protest, but Silas puts up a single finger.

"Do not push me, Isadora. I found a way to tether you to this bookshop and, like any transmutation, I am certain it can be reversed."

A ripple of shock flutters through her ghostly image and she vanishes through the wall, into the apartment.

I step back and gaze at Silas with concern. "Whoa! That was harsh. You know she always means well."

He removes his glasses and slips them back into his pocket. His eyes fill with regret and worry. "Your grandmother is as dear to me as a sister, but neither of you seems to appreciate the true depth of danger presented by Mr. Bombay. The things I teach you are not party tricks; they may one day save your life—or that of someone you love." His eyes grow misty and he turns away.

Hesitantly, I place a hand on his shoulder and ask, "Who did you lose?"

A wave of emotion passes through him, and I feel it as if it were my own.

He pulls out a chair and drops into it like a half-empty sack of potatoes.

I plunk myself down on the floor at his feet, like an acolyte of Plato, and wait in somber silence.

"It was long before you were a twinkle in your mother's eye. I was young, headstrong, and full of pride. I'd recently passed my bar exam with flying colors and proposed to my sweetheart. Our nuptials were scheduled for the first day of May. Her family wanted a June wedding, but for she and I, May first held a special meaning." He pulls a handkerchief from one of his many pockets and dabs at his eyes.

Fighting the urge to interrupt, I force myself to save my questions for later.

"She was a lovely woman, but as far from traditional as one could wander in those days. She loved adventure and convinced me to take her canoeing on the Cree River. Precipitation had been unusually fortuitous that year, and the river was running high and fast. A man with more intelligence and less bravado would've put his foot down and refused." Once again, he wipes the tears leaking from the corners of his eyes.

Every part of me knows that his story has a horrible ending, but once you pull your finger out of the dam, there's no putting it back in.

"We launched the canoe at about 9:00 a.m. and had a rough and exciting paddle until we pulled off on a sandy beach to enjoy the liverwurst sandwiches she'd packed." He smooths his mustache with thumb and forefinger. "The bread was home-made. She reached toward me to brush the crumbs from my chin." He exhales slowly. "Grizzlies still roamed far south, back in the day, and a large male burst from the forest and charged. Whether he was protecting his territory or hungry, we didn't wait to find out. We abandoned our supplies and ran for the canoe."

"Did you make it?" I only have so much self-control.

"We did, and as we paddled with all our strength, pulling away from the angry beast, a wave of relief washed over both of us. That relief carried with it a lack of focus. I failed to hear the rushing water approaching, and when the canoe entered the swirling rapids we were tossed to and fro like rag dolls."

Now I have to wipe tears from my eyes.

"I grabbed onto a fallen tree, which stretched over the abyss, and watched the canoe smash against boulders and splinter into a hundred pieces. I called out for her, but there was no reply." He takes a ragged breath. "I made my way to the bank and searched every boulder in the rapids. She was nowhere to be found. I continued my desperate search downstream, and in a quiet eddy, under a budding willow tree, I saw her green dress floating like watercress on the surface. I charged into the river and grabbed her. I dragged her to shore, but—"

I place my hand on his knee and let my tears flow freely.

"A loss of breath, water in the lungs, those things I could have attended. But the brutal rocks and the thundering water had battered her beyond repair. It took me two days to hike to civilization, carrying her broken body."

"I'm so sorry."

"Her family never forgave me, and I never forgave myself. Decades later, when I met your grandmother and we began our exploration into alchemy, I found healing in the power of transmutation." He wipes his eyes one final time and returns the hanky to his pocket, before placing a gnarled hand on top of mine and gazing into my soul. "If I teach you how to protect yourself, to prevent such heartache in your own life, I will have found a way to honor her passing. Perhaps now you understand the gravity of the information I wish to share?"

My voice is lost to the knot gripping my throat and the tears spilling down my cheeks. I nod vigorously.

Silas pats my hand and takes the blood-red book from the table. He hands it to me.

I take the book, still unable to speak, and nod fervently.

He demonstrates the two remaining symbols.

I repeat his motions with careful reverence.

"Practice tracing the symbols in water, or perhaps coffee, until you feel the veil lift and you see the truth."

Nodding, I cradle the book to my chest.

He rises and quietly leaves the bookshop.

CHAPTER 15

AFTER PRACTICING the symbols for a day and a half, and sustaining myself on frozen pizza and Fruity Puffs, bedtime has finally arrived.

I lie on my four-poster bed, enveloped in the scent of my new lavender pillow spray—staring at the ceiling.

Tossing and turning, I throw the covers off. I flip the pillow over. I stack three pillows under my head. I pull the covers back on.

Finally, I admit defeat and sit up. "I need a drink."

A blur of ghostly energy whizzes toward me. "Careful, young lady. That's how it starts. First you need a drink to fall asleep. Then you need a drink to relax. Next it's a drink to loosen up. Before you know it, you're trapped in an endless loop, searching for a life at the bottom of a bottle."

"Grams, I respect your struggle. I do. And I know that alcoholism is a disease, but I'm not an alcoholic."

She crosses her bejeweled limbs and looks away.

"Seriously, Grams. I may have been a bit of a drinker back in Arizona, but ever since I came to Pin Cherry, I've been too busy getting in and out of trouble to care about drinks. Mostly. I'm taking it one day at a time, all right."

Grams uncrosses her arms and mumbles, "Don't mock my mantras."

"Mock your mantras? Is that anything like flippant forays?"

She smiles, in spite of her pout, and swirls closer. "I love that man to death, but he can be so intense!"

The wave of punchiness that follows exhaustion hits me like a locomotive. "You did love him to death!" I giggle uncontrollably. "Yours!"

"Oh, Mitzy, you're too much!" She joins me in another round of whoops and hollers.

"Reeeee-ow." A warning.

"Uh oh. We've disturbed Mr. Cuddlekins." Grams snorts and covers her grin with a ring-ensconced hand.

"If you think he's upset now, wait till he finds out that I ate all his Fruity Puffs!" I double over with belly laughs.

"REE-ow!" The sound of imminent retribution.

I leap onto the bed and pull the thick down comforter over my head.

A moment later a heavy thud lands on top of me, and a sharp THWACK of warning hits my backside.

I peek cautiously above the edge of the duvet. "I promise to respect the claw, Pye. I'll run to the store first thing in the morning and restock your cupboard."

He turns and performs the yoga move we refer to as "downward D-word" and stretches across two-thirds of the bed.

The laughter and horseplay turns the tide. And before I can say "Pyewacket," the strong fingers of sleep reach up and pull me into the depths.

When morning comes too soon, I decide on a lighthearted T-shirt that displays a hammer and a pile of nails below the phrase, "This is Not a Drill." Additionally, I take a couple of extra minutes to get ready since I'll be heading out to Fox Mountain immediately after I feed the beast.

. . .

The ski lodge looks more dilapidated than ever in the harsh winter sun, and there's no additional enthusiasm inside. The distracted desk clerk informs me that Brandy is in her cottage. No eye contact and no directions.

I head back outside and follow the signs to the little cabin.

Brandy answers on the first knock, but her expression is not one of welcome.

"Hey, do you have a minute?"

"Just." She doesn't budge.

"Can I come in?"

She moves a fraction of an inch. "What do you want, Mitzy? I have a pounding headache and a million things to do."

Geez. Drunk Brandy is way nicer than sober Brandy. "I just wanted to offer my condolences. I'm sorry about Oliver."

Her gaze narrows and her teeth grind. "What are you talking about?"

"Didn't the sheriff tell you? They identified the body we found. It was Oliver Kedrowski." I'd love to add that he was clearly staying in room 237, but I'd rather not incriminate myself.

"What's it to me?" She crosses her arms and glares at me.

"Wasn't he your boyfriend? I thought you might be upset."

Her arms fall to her sides. “Who told you that?”

No time like the present to use an alcoholic’s own fuzzy memories against them. “You did.”

She shifts her weight from one foot to the other and takes a step back. “I would . . . I never . . . That’s not possible.”

I smile warmly and double down. “The other night when we were having drinks you told me that you gave Oliver a love potion. Remember?”

“What?” She paces into her kitchen and presses a hand to her forehead. “No. I don’t remember . . .”

“You said you got the potion from some gypsy woman.”

She turns, wipes her forehead several times, and wrings her hands. “No, that’s not true.”

“Oh. Where did you get the potion then?”

Her breathing is erratic. “I’m not supposed to say.” Her eyes dart around the kitchen. “He wasn’t supposed to die!”

“It was an accident. You have to tell the police, Brandy.”

Like lightning, she reaches in a drawer and pulls a gun. Aiming at my head she warns, “I have a daughter to protect, okay. He wasn’t supposed to die. He was supposed to love me and do what I said.” Her hand shakes and the gun wobbles dangerously. “It all went wrong.”

I step backward toward the door. “The police

will understand. It's always better to come forward and tell the truth before they arrest you."

She jerks the tip of the gun toward the hallway. "No one is going to tell the police anything. Start walking."

I put my hands up like an actor in a stagecoach robbery reenactment. "I'm here to help you, Brandy."

"No. No. You're lying to me. You were in on it from the beginning." She reaches for a doorknob and opens a door to reveal a narrow, dark staircase.

I want to ask what she thinks I was in on, but the shadowy staircase makes my skin crawl. "What's down there?"

"It's a basement. Get down there. Now."

A basement! That's exactly where every person in every horror movie I've ever watched gets killed. In fact, I think there's even one called *The Basement*! "I'm not going down there, Brandy."

She pulls the hammer back on the revolver. "Go!"

I'm not about to test her mental stability. I run down the steps.

The door slams behind and I hear the distinct clunk of a deadbolt driving home. Would you be surprised to learn that there's no knob on my side? I can almost hear the suspenseful music crescendo.

I feel my way down the stairs and am relieved to

see a sliver of light on the far wall. Rushing toward it, I trip on some junk and hit the ground.

Sitting up slowly, I choose to wait until my eyes fully adjust to the dim cellar.

Once I see the jumble of boxes and bags, I'm way more worried about giant rodents than masked horror-movie villains.

The odors of dust, damp, and decay only add to my anxiety.

Threading a careful path to the window, I stack up three of the strongest looking boxes and peer through the narrow pane of grimy glass.

Even without a measuring tape, I can assure you that these hips will not fit through that window.

A sudden realization dawns like Gandalf arriving on the fifth day. Apologies to the non-nerds; rest assured it was a big "all our problems are pretty much solved" kind of deal. I smack myself on the forehead with the heel of my hand.

You have a phone, idiot!

Making immediate use of my pocket-sized savior, I call for back up. "Hey, Erick, it's Mitzy. Remember how you told me to stay out of this case? Right. So, I didn't do that. And Brandy Hammer locked me in her basement at gunpoint, and I was kinda wondering if you could maybe see your way clear to send a deputy by to let me out?"

I have to hand it to him for keeping his cool. He

calls in the request for assistance before he even chews me out.

Don't get me wrong, he absolutely chews me out. But I think it's important to note how he prioritized my safety before my lecture. I end the call with a humble apology and slip my phone back inside the pocket of my coat.

Sitting down on the boxes, I stare aimlessly at the piles and piles of stuff. The first thing to catch my eye is a mass of skis and assorted outdoor equipment.

You'd think that stuff would be upstairs and not in this creepy, dank basement covered in dust. Upon closer inspection, I deduce that the gear belongs to a man. Going out on a limb, I assume it's her dead husband's.

I guess she couldn't get rid of it, so she piled it down here. But the next thing I notice leaves me with a dry mouth and a sick feeling in my stomach.

Under the rickety stairs, illuminated by the single shaft of light swirling with the mysterious dust I stirred up when I fell, is a small pink blanket. The tattered blanket is surrounded on three sides with stuffed animals, broken dolls, and chipped teacups.

I bend and run my finger over one of the tiny saucers and hold it to the light.

No dust.

I'm starting to worry that I'm not the first person Brandy has locked in her basement. Perhaps I underestimated her lack of stability, and her drinking problem.

I take pictures on my phone, before continuing to snoop through this haunting hideaway.

Carefully opening one of the cardboard boxes on top of a leaning-tower-of-Pisa stack, I unearth a pile of old photographs.

Nice. This will definitely provide some needed distraction.

The people look unfamiliar, until I stumble onto a cross-country ski-team photo. In the middle of the picture is Brandy Schloss—twice.

Multiplicity! Brandy has a twin!

As an only child and, for more than half a decade, an orphan, I've always been fascinated by twins. What would my life have been like if I'd had a twin? Would we have been able to stay together in the foster system? Would she have been identical, like Brandy's twin, or maybe a fraternal twin? What would I be like as a guy?

Oh, the possibilities are endless.

As I move my hand to toss the photo back in the pile, my eyes are drawn to the small, nearly invisible face at the end of the lineup.

No! It can't be! I tap the light on my phone, aim it at the photo, and stare at the tiny face. That is definitely Rory Bombay! I wish there was a handy list of names at the bottom of this pic. No such luck. Regardless, my mood ring is humming with confirmation.

Why did she act like she didn't know him in the bar? I mean, judging by the picture he was rather unmemorable in high school. But I feel like this town's not that big. You wouldn't just forget a teammate, would you?

I head back to the pile of photos and dig down a few additional layers. I've plowed through another hundred photographs by the time I find the memorial program.

Candy Schloss, the twin. Poor girl died at nineteen.

Whoa!

Rifling through a few images of crying attendees, I see the tattered, yellow edge of the newspaper clipping that every fiber of my being knows will be there. The article takes a somber tone, but shows a photo of a smiling Candy in her ski gear.

She died in a terrible skiing accident. The entire county was shocked. Candy was on pace to join the Olympic team. No one could explain how such a talented skier would make such an amateur mistake. As I read the story of Candy's accident . . . Full-moon ski . . . Moose comes out of nowhere . . . Neck broken instantly . . .

The story in the newspaper article sounds exactly like the accident that killed Brandy's husband, Jeffrey.

There are three more photos from the memorial service and, in the final one, I see that sadly forgettable face of a young Rory Bombay, streaked with tears.

I flick the corner of the photo with my finger. So, *Candy* was the high-school crush.

My ring finally offers up some assistance, as the hairs on the back of my neck tingle, and the image from Candy's memorial program swirls inside the glass dome of my mood ring.

Pondering the idea that Candy's death may not have been an accident, and possibly neither was Jeffrey's, my time in Brandy Hammer's basement is beginning to put me on edge.

A smashing sound from above is either a deputy coming to my rescue or Brandy getting ready to add another body to her list of mysterious disappearances.

Whatever misgivings I had about pinning Oliver Kedrowski's murder on the widow Brandy have vanished.

"Miss Moon, respond."

Great, it's my lucky day. Erick sent my number one fan, Deputy Paulsen.

"Down here, Paulsen." I fold the ski-team

photo, the news clipping, and Candy's memorial program and shove everything into my pocket.

"Stand clear, I have to shoot out the lock."

I doubt very seriously she has to shoot the lock. This whole place is falling apart, and I'm certain that the wooden doorframe would crumble under her weight. But let's not split hairs.

I step to the side just as a gunshot echoes through the small basement.

She kicks the door open for good measure and descends three steps. "You do realize we have a whole county to protect."

I shrug. "Feels good to fire that gun though, doesn't it, Deputy?"

She may be able to control her outward expression, but my extra senses pick up on the thrill racing just beneath her skin.

"Do you need me to chauffeur you back to town, too?"

"No thanks, Deputy. I've got my car here. So, now that I'm out, I can take it from here." I gesture to the firearm, which she still hasn't holstered. "You'd make a heckuva locksmith though."

Despite her disdain for me, I hear a muffled chuckle escape from her throat.

Upstairs, a deputy whom, oddly enough, I haven't met, is taking measurements and photographs.

"There's a gun in that drawer under the toaster, if you wanna bag that."

He looks at me and squints.

"That one, right there." I point and nod encouragingly.

He opens the drawer and whips his head back toward me with a look of shock on his face.

"I didn't lock myself in the basement for fun." I grin and head out the door as Deputy Paulsen shoves me forward.

Boy, oh boy, do I have some tidbits for the folks back home.

CHAPTER 16

On my adrenaline-fueled drive back to Pin Cherry Harbor, my phone rings and the lovely Erick Harper has some follow-up questions for me.

Once we clear up the loose ends from my temporary imprisonment in the basement, our discussion moves to the medical examiner's report and the unidentified toxin in Oliver's system.

I remind Erick about the love potion and update him on both Brandy's admission that Oliver wasn't supposed to die, and also my new suspicions of child abuse.

Someone walks into his office and interrupts our call, so he doesn't ask me to text him the photos I took in the basement, but before I hang up, I encourage him to pull the file for Candy's accidental death.

And I text him the photos. He'll thank me later.

I don't think I'll be returning to Fox Mountain. At least not while it's under its current ownership. But one thing I know for certain: Silas and I are definitely going to pay a little visit to that gypsy woman.

A quick call to my mentor sets up our meeting at the bookshop.

A split second after I end that call, a moose walks out of the thick tree cover lining the road.

I slam on my brakes and feel a combination of fear, astonishment, and a heaping helping of gratitude that the roads are clear. The tires grip the pavement and screech, but I successfully come to a halt—a mere car length from the massive mammal.

The moose is completely unimpressed by my incredible driving skills. He turns and looks at me, and my first thought is, "I could hang a hammock between those antlers!"

He saunters across the road and I shudder to think what would've happened to me, or him, if conditions had been less favorable.

With my heart still racing, I ease my foot off the brake and choose to make the rest of the trip at ten miles per hour below the speed limit.

Silas is waiting for me at the Bell, Book & Candle, and before I jump into the tale of my life-threatening run-in with Brandy Hammer, I entertain him and Grams with my "near-miss moose."

He breathes a heavy sigh, and Grams shakes her head but pats her heart in relief.

I take a little bow and press on. "Now, for the less delightful news."

Grams drifts down to eye level before she asks, "Something worse than that happened today?"

I exhale comically. "Have you met me?" After a quick catch-up on the murderous Brandy Hammer's twisted past and sketchy present, I share my idea about visiting the gypsy.

"Absolutely. You march right in there and call her out for being a swindling fraud." Grams punctuates her instruction with a sharp handclap.

"What if she knew the potion was deadly? What if she's selling murder?"

Silas is not as quick to get on board. "While I am in agreement that Ania Karina Nowak and this potion must be dealt with, I feel a more subtle approach is prudent. The fact remains, despite the amateur nature of the vast majority of her prior workings, with the proper resources she poses a genuine threat. If she is somehow connected to the disappearance of *Saducismus Triumphatus*, she is quite likely the person who enchanted that charm bracelet with the witch's bottle spell. We would be wise to assume that her skills have increased over the years and approach with due caution."

"All right, 'due caution' it is. But let's get after it. I just know Rory is in cahoots with her, and I'd like to hear her side of the story before I launch my counterattack on Mr. Bombay."

Grams arches a perfectly drawn brow. "Counterattack?"

"It's a figure of speech. I just mean that there's going to be some retribution."

Silas chuckles and smooths his mustache. "I'm not entirely certain you have a full grasp of the term 'figure of speech.'"

He and Grams share a lengthy chuckle.

"Look, you two, Rory crossed the line. I don't know what he's hiding, and I don't know what he and Brandy are up to, but I'm going to get to the bottom of it and I'm going to make sure he pays for using me."

"That does seem fair, dear." Grams nods her approval.

"Shall we take your vehicle, Mitzy?"

"Always."

Silas and I traverse the whole of Pin Cherry Harbor to arrive at the small retail establishment and homestead of the gypsy, located on the outskirts of the far side of town.

"Is this one of those scenarios where you're going to do all of the talking?"

Silas shakes his head and takes a deep breath. "I am under the impression that this will be a teaching moment."

"Oh, brother." I roll my eyes and exit the vehicle.

"Be on your guard," he whispers, when I reach the front door.

As the door opens, it brushes against a small wind chime and sends the tinkling notes of arrival throughout the small, shadowy shop. The aromas of a multitude of herbs and tinctures fill my nostrils. It's a heady combination.

The shelves are lined with candles, crystals, bundles of dried herbs, small wooden boxes, decks of tarot cards, and on and on. I feel as though I've stepped through a portal and landed right back in Sedona! This place could pass for any one of the crystal-crunching shops in and around uptown.

A hunched, elderly woman, supporting herself on an intricately carved cane, hobbles out from behind a beaded curtain.

It's a cliché, I agree, but you and I both knew there was a beaded curtain.

"Welcome to Ania's Emporium. How may I enlighten your journey?" Her thick Polish accent is difficult to understand.

By the time she reaches the end of the sentence she's shambled close enough to recognize Silas and, certainly, to suspect my identity.

She pulls a small glass vial from her pocket and holds it aloft. "I command you to leave this place."

"Mrs. Nowak, we come in peace. You may put away the banishing hex." Silas lifts one hand and traces a symbol, which I do not recognize, in the air.

She shies away from it, like a horse that has seen a rattlesnake, and shoves the little glass bottle into the pocket of her delicately embroidered cloak. "Do not threaten me with your stolen powers, wizard. This is my shop. My protections prevail."

Silas nods. "Indeed they do. That alone should offer evidence of the purity of our intentions."

She spits on the ground. "Speak your business, and be gone."

When she says, "be gone," I feel a pressure on my chest pushing me back and an icy chill on the ring finger of my left hand.

"Mrs. Nowak, my name is Mitzy Moon. I'm wondering if you remember selling a love potion to Brandy Hammer, the owner of Fox Mountain Ski Resort?"

Her rheumy eyes wander back and forth in their sunken sockets as she leafs through the pages of her memory, searching for the name. "I know no such woman."

"Well that's not—"

Silas puts a firm hand on my arm and intervenes. "Perhaps Miss Moon asks the wrong question, madam. Have you crafted such a potion recently?"

"There are many such potions, wizard. What was the purpose?"

Silas looks to me and shrugs.

"This particular potion was going to be given to a man, and it was most likely meant to compel him to do as the woman desired, or maybe commanded. Either way it was supposed to manipulate this guy."

The gypsy woman makes a strange noise in her throat, which could be disgust or agreement. "I may have crafted such a thing for a regular client. What business is it of yours?"

Ignoring the ring of ice on my finger, I continue, "Well, the victim—"

Silas grips my arm with considerable force. "Thank you. And one last question. Have you recently charmed any bracelets?"

The woman's curved spine straightens and her sunken eyes glitter with defiance. "You underestimate me, wizard. I am not what you call a fraud."

Silas relaxes his grip on my arm and brings both of his hands together to form a circle. He whispers "Odsłoń" as he violently separates his hands—breaking the circle.

The gypsy gasps and drops her cane as a driven wind rushes through her shop. Behind her, to the left, a piece of the wall vanishes, and there on a previously hidden shelf rests my precious copy of *Saducismus Triumphatus*.

"My book! You thieving, no good gypsy!"

"No time, Mitzy. Retrieve it at once," Silas commands.

I hurry past the gypsy woman, grab a small step stool, climb up, and rescue my tome. The second the book is safely in my hands, the wall resumes its solidity and I fall backward in shock. Fortunately, I was only a couple of steps up in the air and I easily live to tell the tale. Thank heavens for padding in all the right places!

Mrs. Nowak reaches for her cane and comes up fighting.

Silas makes some other weird gestures with his hand and her staff flies across the room.

Now I'm fully terrified, because I'm in the middle of a *Lord of the Rings* style battle between Gandalf and Saruman.

Clearly, Silas can take care of himself.

Running out of the shop, I jump in my Jeep and start the engine.

Silas follows a moment later looking victorious but exhausted. As soon as he closes his door, I floor-it out of that place, spitting gravel like Bo Duke.

"Let's hope I never have to come back here."

Silas places a hand on his chest and takes several labored breaths. "Indeed."

Once the dangerous gypsy's shop is out of sight, I pull over. "What do you need? How can I help?"

Silas nods. "Perhaps, if you could give me just a moment."

I reach for a mostly frozen bottle of water on the back seat and hand it to him. "Maybe drink a little water."

"Yes." He takes the bottle and sips what little melted ice there is. He recaps the bottle and presses the frozen liquid to his temple. "Let's get some lunch."

"Copy that." I push my winter driving skills to their limit as I race toward Myrtle's Diner.

I severely underestimated Silas Willoughby, and I will not make that mistake again. Whatever he wants me to learn, I will learn it. Whatever he wants me to read, I will read it. This old guy is my new hero.

Once his breathing returns to normal, I have a few questions for him.

"What was that spell you used back there?"

He takes a sip of water before answering. "It was not a spell, Mitzy. Words have power. If you ask me for money and I say 'yes,' that word has an effect on you. If you ask me for money and I say 'no,' that word has a different effect. Using the right word, and combining it with a powerful intention, produces the desired effect."

His response ventures farther into the philosophical than I had hoped, and only gives me more questions than answers. "All right. What was that word, though? Usually your words sound more Latin-y, that one sounded kind of Russian, or maybe Swedish?"

"Your ear will improve over time, but you are correct in deducing that the word does not come from the Latin. There is power in using one's native tongue, and since Mrs. Nowak is Polish, I believed that she would have used a Slavic incantation to conceal the stolen item. My choice of using a Polish word to see behind her ruse proved a fortunate postulation."

"How many languages do you speak?"

Silas smooths his mustache and gazes out the window. "Fluently, only four. However, my studies led me to uncover the power of reading texts in their original language, rather than clumsy translations. In addition to those four, I have a working knowledge of at least nine others."

"Wow. Which ones do you speak?"

He chuckles. "English, German, Gaelic, and Bauan."

"Come again? What was that last one?"

"Bauan is the official Fijian dialect. Each island has its own twist, some very similar and others quite different. But with a working knowledge of Bauan Fijian, one can read most of the printed literature and communicate effectively with the majority of the islands' inhabitants."

There's a whole side to Silas that I never envisioned. In my mind he spent his entire life in Pin Cherry Harbor, but the reality sounds a lot more interesting. "Have you ever been to Fiji?"

"Several times. Beautiful people, with a rich and complicated history. But my days of globetrotting are behind me." He sighs, and my extra senses pick up on feelings of longing and nostalgia.

Cut to a classic Mitzy Moon left-field distraction. "I can't believe we got it back!" I smack my hand on the steering wheel. "You were amazing in there!"

"I did what was necessary to recover an important text. And she was correct about one implication. I have underestimated her, and she is no longer the fraud your grandmother once thought. However, I do have a growing concern about these 'regular clients' she mentioned."

Once again, an icy chill encircles the ring finger of my left hand, and I glance down just in time to see two devious green eyes blink and disappear. "Like Rory Bombay?"

"Indeed."

"We know she's the one who put the *charm* in my charm bracelet. Do you think she made that potion for him as well?"

"Since you have uncovered a past link between Mr. Bombay and Mrs. Hammer, it is possible that they were working together to make sure Mr. Kedrowski's story was published. Perhaps Mr. Bombay assisted her out of some sense of loyalty to her late sister."

I admire his impulse to believe Rory's intentions may have been good, but something doesn't add up. "Unfortunately, my powers were trapped in that witch's bottle bracelet thingy the first time I was with both of them in the bar. I can't be sure of the authenticity of her reactions—or his. I was blissfully unaware."

He sighs. "You felt relief when your powers were blocked."

"I felt different. At first I think it was relief. The messages, feelings, visions . . . Sometimes it's too much. But once I saw what it was like to be stripped of them . . . Let's just say, I'd rather know too much than have the wool pulled over my eyes by the likes of Rory Bombay!"

I park the Jeep in front of Myrtle's and offer Silas my arm as he exits the vehicle.

"Thank you, Mitzy. I am still not fully myself, and I believe I would benefit from your support."

Leave it to Silas to make it sound so formal. I chuckle as I hold the door for him.

Odell salutes us through the orders-up window and a moment later visits our table.

"Sounds like you got yourself into a little kerfuffle this morning." He laughs and winks.

"Let me guess, Deputy Paulsen?"

"The one and only. The way she told the story made it sound like you broke into Brandy's house or something."

I open my mouth in shock. "Broke in? Not even close. I went out there, as a friend, and the next thing you know, Brandy pulled a gun on me and forced me downstairs."

Odell's brown eyes darken, and the wrinkles around his mouth deepen as he frowns. "I don't like the sound of that one bit."

"Trust me, neither did I. Luckily I had my phone, and Erick was kind enough to send a patrol car out to check on things." That version of the story definitely helps me sound a little less incompetent.

"You've got a real knack for gettin' yourself in trouble." Odell raps his knuckles on the table and walks back into the kitchen.

I look across the silver-flecked surface at Silas and shrug. "What's our next move?"

Silas steeples his fingers and bounces his chin on the tip of his index fingers. "Perhaps a test is in order."

Not sure if he means for me or someone else, so I'm hesitant to throw my support behind his idea. "What kind of test?"

Odell slides two cups of coffee on the table and hurries back to the grill.

Silas pushes his cup of coffee toward me. "The symbols."

I scrunch up my face and look from him to the coffee and back. "Should I draw them on the cup?

"You must infuse them, and their power, directly into the fluid."

For someone who's such a stickler for manners, I find it hard to believe that he's encouraging me to put my finger in his coffee. "All right, but I want you to remember that you told me to do this."

He nods imperceptibly and ceases bouncing his chin. He is still as a statue, waiting for me to complete his challenge.

I put my finger into the coffee, draw each symbol with slow and measured strokes, and hold my open hand over the cup for a moment before I slide it across the table.

Silas picks up the mug of coffee and takes a

long, thoughtful sip. He sets down the cup and looks at me.

Leaning forward eagerly, I ask, "Did it work? Can I ask you anything?"

"Do you believe that it worked?"

I shrug. "I'm not sure."

"Then you are correct."

Dagnabbit! Silas and his answering questions with questions and riddles. In my heart, I receive his meaning. If I don't believe in the transmutation, then I can be certain it did not work. Like he told me on the way over, words have power but they need to be combined with the proper intention.

"I need more practice."

He takes another sip of coffee and holds onto the cup. "Now that I believe."

"Touché."

Odell sets our food on the table and puts a hand on my shoulder. "I, for one, am pretty happy Paulsen rescued you. Even if she rubbed your nose in it a little, still worth it." He sniffs, runs a hand over his utilitarian buzz cut, and leaves us to enjoy our food.

CHAPTER 17

My night spent tossing and turning in my bed was filled with magical battles and secret potions. My morning will be consumed with downing coffee, stealing Fruity Puffs, and setting up the murder wall.

"Need any help?" Grams sparkles into existence next to me and curtsies.

"Perfection, Grams." I roll the wheeled corkboard, which Twiggy has provided to keep me from damaging the lath and plaster walls, into the middle of the room. "Make cards for Brandy, Rory, and Harold Doherty."

Grams busies herself with the intense concentration necessary to move the physical pen and mark the 3 x 5 cards.

I pin up Candy Hammer's memorial service program, the old newspaper article about her death, and the ski team photo.

"Done!"

I turn, and one completed card is floating in midair, gripped between Grams insubstantial thumb and forefinger.

"Thank you." I pin the "Brandy Schloss Hammer" card up and run a length of green yarn from her to the team pic and the program. We have to use green yarn instead of red, because red is "too morbid" for Grams. Imagine, a ghost who's afraid of blood.

"I can hear you, dear."

"Focus more on writing cards and less on listening in, Missy!"

She laughs and floats me another card.

For a moment, I toy with the idea of lighting the "Rory Bombay" card on fire, but I swallow my disgust and tack the card at the opposite end of the board. He gets a connection to the team photo, the program, and to Brandy.

"There!"

Taking the "Harold Doherty" card, I pin it up. No connections—yet.

"What's next, dear?"

My impatience gets the best of me, and I take

over the card-writing duties. Jeffrey (the dead husband), Land Survey, Natural Resources Department, Legacy Land, Oliver Kedrowski, and Thieving Gypsy each get a card tacked on the murder wall.

Once I finish making all the connections, that I know about, one thing stands out. Oliver Kedrowski had no connection to Rory. His death had to be an accident. But the ME's report said "toxin" not "allergen."

"You'll figure it out. Aren't you getting any messages?"

The sullen black swirls in my magicked mood ring offer nothing. "The only message I'm getting is a rumbly in my tumbly! A girl can only do so much on a stolen handful of sugary cereal."

"RE-ow." Feed me.

"Yes, Pye. I will take care of your needs first, as always." I run a hand through my haystack of white hair. "But then I need sustenance and a proper cup of liquid alert."

As I sit at the counter in the diner, I can't take my eyes off the front page. There's a haunting photo of the run-down Fox Mountain Ski Resort and the headline reads, "Murder On The Mountain?" I've got to give it to Quince and his father for getting ahead of the story. But there's not much concrete information in the article.

Brandy was taken in for questioning. No mention of the daughter or the grandmother. I'll have to try my luck with mining additional details from my law-enforcement sources.

The diner is nearly empty, and I doubt the old-timer at the table by the window could hear me if I shouted directly into his ear, so I figure it's safe to speak freely. "Odell, do you remember when Candy Hammer was killed?"

He glances up to the right and nods his head slowly. "Big accident, something to do with a moose, I think."

"That's the story I heard. She went night skiing under a full moon and a moose walked out unexpectedly, etcetera. Just seems odd, you know. She was rumored to be such a talented skier, on her way to the Olympic team. Seems like she would've had time to swerve. Right?"

"I don't know a whole lot about skiing, Mitzy. But I seem to recall some hushed stories about a cover-up. But who's to say?"

"A cover-up? Like maybe it wasn't an accident?"

"Hold on a minute." He disappears, and a moment later Tally returns early from her break.

She walks out and leans down, speaking in secretive tones. "There was a story, back in the day. I hate to repeat it, but it sure made more sense than that tall-tale they told at that poor little girl's memorial service."

Ooh, small town gossip. "What was the story?"

Tally whispers conspiratorially, "I heard from one of the girls that used to work at the salon that Candy and Brandy were skiing together that night and it was Brandy who ran into the moose. You know she wasn't near as good a skier as her sister. But she didn't break her neck or anything. She just made that big moose real angry. So he musta come after her, you know, charged or whatever."

"Really?"

"That's what I heard."

"How is it that Candy is the one who died?"

"Well, the lady that does the hair and makeup on them, you know—"

"Corpses?"

"I wouldn't speak ill of the dead, for sure. Anyhow, she said the family didn't want any hair or makeup done for Candy. She said they wouldn't let anybody see the body. And they had that closed-casket memorial service for a very different reason, not some pish tosh about respect for the dead."

I can't help but lean forward. "What was the real reason?"

Tally leans so close her tightly bound, flame-red

bun bumps my head. “The cousin of the man who runs the groomer on the slopes said there was blood everywhere. Like somebody had spilled a fifty-gallon drum of red paint on that slope. They say Candy went after that moose with a ski pole to try to save her sister, and that moose didn’t take too kindly to it. Have you seen the size of their antlers! I don’t know what that little girl was thinkin’. But he must’ve turned on her—just ripped her up something terrible. Bless her poor little heart, trying to save her sister. God rest her.”

She stands up, crosses her arms, and shakes her head with sadness and regret. “You know I love my sister Tilly to death, but I’m not entirely sure I would take on a bull moose for her.” Tally picks up an errant pencil from the counter, shoves it in her bun, and returns to the kitchen.

I sit back and take several sips of coffee. Who knows how much truth there is in those rumors, but that sure makes a lot more sense than the sanitized version I heard. It would also clear Brandy of any malicious involvement. But a thing like that would definitely affect a person. Maybe I’ll saunter over to the police station and see if Erick’s heard this story.

Furious Monkeys is hard at work leveling up on her favorite game, but she actually pauses and looks up at me. “He’s interrogating that Hammer woman from the lodge. You can wait in his office.”

"Thanks, Baird." You'll note I use her proper name. I mean, I can't exactly call her Furious Monkeys to her face. Pushing on through the familiar territory, I give a congenial nod to the two deputies at their desks, get myself a glass of water from the water cooler, and take a seat in Erick's office.

I can barely hear what's going on in the room across the hall and I wonder if there's an observation room on the other side of the one-way glass.

Peeking out of the office, I check the hall to make sure it's all clear and open the unmarked door between Interrogation Room One and Two.

Finally, a movie trope that does not disappoint! There's an observation room with one-way glass on either side, looking into Interrogation Room One on one side and Interrogation Room Two on the other. There's even an old black and white CRT monitor showing closed-circuit feed from inside the room.

I press the silver switch above the speaker and voilà! I can hear the interrogation.

Brandy is sobbing uncontrollably, and Erick is sitting on the opposite side of the table waiting patiently.

I don't recognize the man sitting next to Brandy, but I assume it's her lawyer.

Closing my eyes, I reach out with my psychic feelers. Her emotion is more than fifty percent genuine, but Erick's mask of patience is only skin-deep.

He slides a glass of water toward her. "Take a drink, Brandy, and pull yourself together. You'll have to answer these questions sooner or later."

She pulls her sleeve down and wipes her eyes, takes a sip of the water, and swallows audibly. "I didn't mean to kill anyone. I swear to you it was just a love potion."

"I understand, but the fact of the matter is, you did kill someone."

The lawyer pipes up, "Allegedly."

Erick ignores the interruption. "And based on the rapid action of the toxin found in the victim's blood work, your potion is the last thing Oliver Kedrowski ingested. So I'll ask you again, where did you get the potion?"

"I told you, he got it from that gypsy woman."

Erick leans toward the recording device on the table. "I'd like to make a note that we will check the transcription to verify. However, I believe you previously stated that you got the potion from the gypsy woman. This is the first I've heard you mention 'he.' Can you please state this person's name for the record?"

Brandy squirms in her chair. "He told me not to say."

Her lawyer leans in and whispers, "You don't have to answer, Mrs. Hammer."

Erick leans towards her, and the intensity of his

stare makes me want to confess to things I've never done. "Hammer, right now you're looking at murder one. If you're covering for someone, now is the time to stop. I'm going to ask you one more time. Who got the potion for you?"

"Rory Bombay."

I gasp, and Erick's eyes dart toward the one-way glass. I slap a hand over my mouth and step back. Even though I'm certain he can't see, somehow he knows.

"Let's take a break, alrighty, Mrs. Hammer?"

She nods and whimpers.

"You need to answer verbally for the tape."

"Yes. I'd like a break."

Her lawyer shuffles some papers, and Erick stops the recording.

I hightail it back into his cramped office before I get busted eavesdropping on his interrogation.

The door opens to Interrogation Room One, and as Erick walks into his office his mouth curves into a half-smile. "Miss Moon. I thought I heard someone snooping around."

"Snooping?"

"What brings you in?"

"I heard some more details about Candy Hammer's death. I was wondering if you could confirm if they're part of the official record?"

He closes his scuffed office door. "Try me."

I fill him in on the rumor about the moose battle and Brandy being present for the whole thing, and wait with all of my senses on high alert for his reaction.

"It sounds like time and overactive imaginations have enhanced the story to near urban legend levels, but the basic facts are correct. Brandy was present. Candy was badly stomped by the moose."

"And Jeffrey?"

"Who?"

"Jeffrey, Brandy's late husband. The one that also died in a moose accident."

Erick scrunches up his face. "Brandy never married."

"All right, partner then. Whatever you want to call the father of Brandy's daughter."

"Sorry, Moon. That's another swing and a miss. She doesn't have any kids."

"But when I mentioned child abuse, you asked me to send you the pictures."

"I don't think I did ask for the pictures. Anyway, I thought you were talking about Brandy. I was distracted."

My head starts spinning. I never actually saw a child. But why would Brandy's mother be there—"So, it's just Brandy and her mother living in that cottage? Why all the men's skiing gear in the basement?"

Erick puts a hand on my shoulder. "Are you sure you're feeling all right? Brandy's mom killed herself in that house a few months after Candy's accident. Brandy lived there with her dad until he died last year. The ski stuff was probably his. What made you think her mother lived there?"

Newsflash: I see ghosts! Plural. Of course, I can't tell Erick about this new development, but now the familiarity of that ghost-hug from Brandy's mother is making a whole lot more sense. Probably best to go with a left-field maneuver. "Are you going to look into that weird set up of 'not dusty' toys in her basement?"

"Honestly, Moon? I'm gonna be a little busy tracking down Rory Bombay and bringing him in for questioning."

I almost forgot to act surprised. Luckily I covered well. "What? What does Rory have to do with this?"

Erick chuckles. "You should go ahead and submit that for the Academy's consideration." He shakes his head. "As I'm sure you heard, Rory is the one who gave her the potion. So if Brandy honestly didn't intend to kill Oliver, maybe Rory had a motive."

"What motive would he have?"

"Brandy was selling the resort to Rory.

"Wait? To Rory?"

Before Erick can answer, an image from the silent movie on the SD card flashes in my mind, and as the man with his back to the camera dives into the shadows, I see a little flash of metal on the pinky finger of his left hand. Now I gotta see that again. Somehow, I need to see that little clip.

"Moon? Where did you go?"

"I think Rory was in negotiations with Harold Doherty. I don't think he was trying to help Brandy as much as she might think. Rory was probably trying to scoop up that property for pennies and then sell it for a fortune to Doherty's development firm."

Erick nods. "I wasn't aware you were acquainted with Harold Doherty. So is that what you took from Oliver's room? The SD card?"

I put my hands up in surrender. "Guilty as charged, Erick. If you let me take another peek at that clip, I think I can prove Rory is the second man in the frame."

"I need to finish questioning Mrs. Hammer. Without further interruption." He tilts his head meaningfully in my direction. "Why not run on over to the newspaper and see if Quince kept a copy."

My eyes widen with mock innocence. "Quince? What makes you think he would have a copy?"

"You two aren't nearly as sneaky as you'd like to

believe." He grins, and I detect a hint of superiority. "I'll talk to you later, Moon. Whether I want to or not, I'd imagine."

For once I take the hint and leave without pushing my luck.

CHAPTER 18

AFTER SUCCESSFULLY AVOIDING ARREST, I swing by the *Pin Cherry Harbor Post* in hopes of getting another look at that clip.

This time, when I enter the last bastion of old-school journalism, the elder Knudsen is behind the front counter. I failed to learn his name on previous visits, but experience has taught me not to ask this man a question unless I have at least thirty minutes to spare.

I keep my query rhetorical. "Quince in the back?" I say, as I point and keep walking.

Blink. Blink. Blink.

His amphibian-sized eyes follow me, like those in a creepy painting in an episode of *Scooby Doo*, as I pass behind the counter and continue into Quince's domain.

Made it!

The chair in front of the computer is empty, so I assume Quince is in the darkroom. I step into the black cylinder and turn, magically revealing the red glow and strong odor of chemical baths.

He looks up. "Hey."

In an effort to speak his language I reply, "Hey."

Walking toward the tray of chemicals, I watch him swish a sheet of photographic paper back-and-forth with rubber-tipped tongs. An image slowly appears, as if by magic. And I guess that's really what science is, isn't it. It's a form of magic that we can explain.

"I need to see that clip of Doherty again."

The tongs abruptly stop moving. "I ditched the SD card at the sheriff's station. That was our deal."

"I'm pretty sure you kept a copy."

"It'll cost you."

"Not so fast, Don Corleone. Let's say I paid in advance when I didn't confirm the sheriff's suspicions that you were the one who slipped that card through the mail slot. Deal?"

"Deal. Don't go aggro."

Stepping back, I scoff. I mean, I did a little gaming in my day. Aggro is an informal term meaning rage or extreme aggravation. Clearly my failure to fork over lots of cash is Quince's equivalent of "aggro." You gotta love this kid's spirit.

He rinses his print and lays it in the drying rack. For those of you keeping score at home, that's another movie trope that fails to deliver. No strings crisscrossing the darkroom. No clips gripping strange photographs. Just a nice, practical drying rack that protects the photographic paper and keeps the images flat.

Quince pops into the ejection tube, and I step back to wait my turn. I'm pretty sure the little cylinder could hold two people, but on previous occasions he's expressed his discomfort with my physical nearness and I have no intention of putting him on edge.

When the cylinder stops, I rotate it back toward me with my hand and climb in. By the time I pop out the other side he's already in front of the computer, clicking and tapping furiously.

He plays the clip. The moment when the man with his back turned to the camera darts into the shadows, his left hand lifts into the light and I see the glint of metal on the pinky finger.

"I know this isn't TV, but how much can you zoom in?"

He chuckles. "Right?"

Quince clicks, grabs another tool, selects the area, clicks again, and the next thing you know—we've got a rather close-up, blurry image of the metal band on flesh.

Since movies and the digital world are kind of more "my realm," I decide to show off. "Hey, slide over."

Quince stares at me in confusion, but as I move toward him he instinctively moves away.

I grab the mouse, open the luma adjustment panel, add a contrast filter, and boost the blacks. I'm pretty impressed with myself, but it's not until I hear Quince mumble an awestruck "Sweet" that I know I've actually accomplished something.

"Looks like a class ring, right?"

"Super old, though."

"Yeah. Super old." Rory did say the ring belonged to his mother, when I noticed it on our drive out to Fox Mountain. I suppose in this high-school kid's world that is super old. I'm sure when I was his age, I thought the same thing. It's funny how each year you get older, your concept of old sort of shifts. I step away from the computer, nod my thanks, and start to leave.

"You want me to print that?"

"Are you offering me a freebie?"

"It's like, a gear drop for those sick computer tricks."

His admiration brings a blush to my cheeks, and I bow. "I'm honored."

He exhales and mumbles something inaudible as he clicks a few buttons.

The printer springs to life.

Grabbing the sheet, I thank him and head back to my Jeep.

No messing around today. I'm going to take this printout straight to Erick. He'll need all the help he can get connecting Rory to Doherty, and this land deal.

Back at the station there's a full manhunt underway for Rory Bombay. Extra deputies have been called in and people are streaming in and out of Erick's office like he's giving away free chocolate samples.

No one even notices me pass through the station, until Erick looks up with a worried frown.

"Hopefully this will put a smile on your face." I lay the printout on his desk. He looks up at me. "Kind of looks like an extremely blurry photo of a Pin Cherry High class ring."

"Erick Harper, for the win."

"Look, Moon, I don't have time for games. What's this mean?"

"That's an enlarged photo, that one of your"—I make air quotes with my fingers—"'deputies' printed out from that clip of Harold Doherty. The one that was discovered on Oliver Kedrowski's SD card."

He holds the image up, looks at me, and looks

back at the image. "And what did my deputy think this would mean to me?"

"That's Rory Bombay's ring. I've seen that ring on his pinky finger."

"It's something, I guess. I appreciate the effort, Moon. I really do. But you gotta know this would never hold up in court. I'll grant you that it's a class ring. Anybody who graduated from that school could have one of these. Maybe he wears a ring on his pinky, maybe he doesn't." Erick drops the photo on his desk and leans back with a frustrated exhale. "Brandy's accusation that Rory coerced her to form a romantic relationship with the journalist isn't enough. She's desperate to shift the blame off her own shoulders, and any jury would see that in a minute. I need hard evidence that connects Rory Bombay directly to Oliver's murder."

"I'll see what I can do." As I leave the room, I get a sharp pain in my temple, and I raise my hand to my head. As soon as I touch my head, the ring on my left hand sizzles with information. The toxin.

I turn back and whisper, "It's the toxin, Erick. You've got to get the ME to run some additional tests and identify the specific mechanism. How it works is the key to figuring out what it is."

Erick stands up slowly, tilts his head, and narrows his gaze. "You got all that from a headache?"

"Oh, weird right." I giggle nervously.

"Yeah, pretty weird." His voice is hollow and his eyes hold a spark of concern.

"Well, I gotta go." I've never rushed out of that police station so quickly. I make a hard left out the front door and break into a brisk jog back to my Jeep.

Weird doesn't begin to describe what just happened. Not only did I get some oddly specific information, but also I basically had a supernatural episode right in front of the local sheriff. So much for keeping my powers a secret!

I burst through the front door of the bookshop in a bit of a tizzy, and a wave of relief washes over me when I see my father. "Dad, I could really use some fatherly advice right now."

He smiles, bends down, and opens his arms to pull me into a bear hug. "Let's hope I've got some."

The more I try to bring him up to speed on the murder, and Rory, and Brandy, and my breaking and exiting, and seeing more ghosts, and my slip up in front of Erick, the more confused he gets.

"Sweetie, let's stop playing catastrophe roulette. Pick one, and I'll do my best."

With a heavy sigh, I lean back against the wall. "I guess my biggest problem is Erick. I mean, I definitely want to pin this murder on Rory—backstabbing snake—but, in the long run, I don't want Erick to think I'm a circus sideshow freak."

Grams whizzes in, and Dad shivers as she passes by him. “Seeing my ghost is old news, dear.”

“Actually, I think I saw another ghost. That night when I escorted a plastered Brandy Hammer back to her cottage, a woman claiming to be Brandy’s mother opened the door.”

Even though they can’t hear each other, Jacob and Grams both ask, “What makes you think she was a ghost?”

“Because Erick just told me that Brandy’s mom committed suicide after Candy’s accident, almost thirty years ago.”

Grams’ floaty form freeze-frames. “In that house?”

I nod.

“Her spirit must be trapped. Could you communicate with her?”

Once again, I nod.

“Maybe you can help her cross over. If that’s what she wants . . .” Grams voice drifts off and she vanishes.

I fill Dad in on the news. “I hope this doesn’t sound too selfish, Dad, but I can deal with this ghost thing later. What do I do about flying my freak flag in front of Erick?”

Grams snaps back into existence like a firecracker. “Erick Harper should be so lucky to have a girl like you. If he doesn't see that, then he's not worth your time, dear."

"Those are brave words, Grams. But in reality, I can't just turn my heart off and on. There's something about him, something I kind of want to get to know better."

Jacob clears his throat. "In my experience, honesty pretty much wins the day. Amaryllis knows that I'm an ex-con, and she knows I want to make amends. She supports me, and the Restorative Justice Foundation, because she believes in giving people second chances.

"I get the honesty thing, Dad. But this isn't normal. It's not like I have a gambling problem, or I'm an alcoholic." I glance at Grams. "No judgment, just an example."

Grams rushes over and places a phantom hand on my arm. "I understand. You absolutely can't tell Erick about your powers."

Did not see that coming. "Grams, are you saying I should lie to him?"

My dad stares at me. "Can you fill me in?"

Holding up a finger, I put my dad on hold while Grams finishes her argument.

"I'm not saying you lie to him, Mitzy. I'm saying you continue to lead with your intellect and let the rest be a mystery."

I explain her position to my father and he

shakes his head. "I can't say I'm in total agreement, but I'm not going to push you. Maybe Isadora's way is the right way. You're a smart girl, Mitzy. So smart, in fact, that I know you'll make the right decision when the time comes."

And now my life is an after-school special. No one's giving me concrete advice. It's all platitudes and nonsense I've seen printed on inspirational posters. "All right, I'll stay the course for now." I smile at Ghost-ma and Dad. "So, you guys think I'm pretty smart?"

My father chuckles. "And modest."

Grams snorts and vanishes through the wall before I can scold her.

"Hey, Grams, do you think Silas knows some kind of summoning spell?"

She does not reappear, but her voice echoes through the bookshop. "I'm sure he's mentioned at least a couple of times, he doesn't do spells."

"Understood. But I've got to find Rory Bombay. Erick needs to bring him in for questioning, and we both know Rory has the means to slip away undetected."

Grams bursts through the wall and her eyes are dancing like sparkling stars. "Oooh, I know this one. Follow me." She launches down the hall, through the floor of the Rare Books Loft, and I'm assuming through the wall to the apartment.

Hustling up the circular staircase and across the loft, I reach up to pull the candle-handle and smile warmly. *Saducismus Triumphatus* is back on the shelf and everything is right with the world. Stepping through the bookcase doorway, I join her as she zips back and forth in front of the built-in bookcases in the apartment.

"Right here. Push right here."

I lean toward one of the carved decorative panels beneath the bookcase and shrug. "You mean this piece of *wall*?"

"Just do as I say."

Wow, I see where Pye gets his snark. I push the panel and jump back in shock as a large drawer slowly emerges from the wall.

"No one thought to mention this until now?"

"The teacher appears when the student is ready." Grams glances through the drawer and points. "There, that pendulum. You need that, and we'll need a map of Pin Cherry Harbor and the surrounding area.

"Copy that. Pendulum and a map." I pick up the item she indicated, and as soon as my left hand comes in contact with the chain my whole arm tingles with energy. "You don't happen to have a secret map drawer in here, do you?"

"I think there's some kind of map book downstairs in the 'Geography' section."

She zooms through the wall while I open the door like a civilized person. Down on the first floor she zips up and down the stacks and I hear her call out, "Here! This will work."

Before I can get the book she's indicating, Pyewacket jumps down from one of his secret high places and drops that blasted frog puppet on my feet.

"Ree-ow." A gentle reminder.

"Yes, Pye. I know you like this plushy, but I don't have time to play right now." I push the green thing aside and walk toward Grams.

"Reeeee-ow." A warning.

"Uh oh," she whispers.

"Don't encourage him, Grams." I kneel down and wag my finger at the spoiled caracal. "Look, mister, the grown-ups are busy right now. I will play with you later. Understood?"

He swipes at my finger—claws out.

Getting to my feet I offer one additional scolding. "I'm not going to reward that behavior."

Making my way to the "Geography" shelves, I pick up the oversized book and follow her glowing apparition to the back room.

"Open it up on the table. Use the zoomed out page."

I flip through the pages until I find one that

shows Pin Cherry Harbor, Fox Mountain, Great Falls, and several other towns I've never heard of.

"Now, you hold the pendulum above the map, by that little loop, and ask it to locate Rory Bombay. Hold the request clear in your mind and don't let anything else interfere. Allow the conical stone hanging from the chain to swing freely until it points to his location."

"Grams, are you serious right now?"

"I believe you kids say 'serious as a heart attack.' Clear your mind. Hold the pendulum. Make your request."

I take a deep cleansing breath. I know, I can't believe it either. Then I hold the pendulum above the map and ask it to locate Rory Bombay.

For a moment nothing happens. Then it swings wildly and a strange energy moves through my hand. Instead of slowing and pointing to a specific location, the pendulum seems to be spiraling out of control. My hand sparks with electricity. I drop the pendulum and step away from the table.

"What the heck, Grams?"

"Maybe he's cloaking himself somehow. Are you sure you asked it to locate Rory Bombay?"

"Yes. Who else would I want to locate?"

"And you cleared your mind of everything else? You didn't let yourself get distracted?"

"I did it right. The dumb thing's just not working."

After several additional unsuccessful attempts, I give up and go upstairs to splash some water on my face.

By the time my arm stops tingling and the flecks of water have evaporated, Grams joins me.

"You did your best, dear."

I don't care for her overtly patronizing tone. "I'm taking a nap."

Grams dematerializes and I flop onto the bed to have a mini pity party.

CHAPTER 19

WHEN I ROLL over to sit on the edge of the bed, Grams is hovering like an impatient thought bubble in a half-finished cartoon strip. I rub my face and exhale my frustration. "What now?"

"You'll have to call Silas, dear. He was always better at these things than me."

A quick call to Mr. Willoughby confirms that, in his opinion, this exercise is beyond my current abilities. He agrees to come straight over.

While we wait for him, I return the pendulum to the mysterious hidden drawer upstairs. Of course, I take the opportunity to examine the rest of its contents.

"What is all this stuff?"

Grams hovers over my left shoulder as she explains. "I was always more interested in the magical side of the occult. Silas found his calling in alchemy, but all of those languages and symbols—they were beyond me."

"Beyond your abilities or your attention span?"

"Mitzy! What are you implying?"

"Nothing really. It's just that you worked your way through an awful lot of husbands. I feel like that points to a slight attention deficit, don't you?"

She laughs and floats over to the large six-by-six windows. Looking out across the ever-thawing waters, she replies, "You may have hit the nail on the head. I preferred to think that I outgrew my partners, and that my constant evolution required new companionship. But in the end, if I'm honest, I suppose I did get bored."

Her wistful tone plucks a chord in my own heart. "I understand, Grams. Life is full of experiences, and with the means to explore them all, I think I would've found it difficult to box myself in too."

She slowly drifts across the room, like an angel on a sunbeam, and a warm smile lights up her face. "I couldn't have put it more beautifully myself. I believe you really are coming to understand the woman I was. I'm so lucky to have a granddaughter like you." Sparkling tears burst from her eyes.

"Grams! Don't start with the waterworks."

We're sharing a tender moment when the bookcase door slides open and Silas bursts in unannounced.

I turn with an instant admonishment. "Hey, Mr. Manners. What happened to knocking or intercoms?"

He shuffles to a stop and his sagging jowls redden. "My apologies. The importance of the task clouded my priorities."

"Take it easy, Silas. I was kidding." I wave away his shame as though I'm shooing a fly. "Do you need a map?"

"That would be prudent."

"Be right back." I hustle down to the back room and grab the oversized map book.

He places it on the coffee table, carefully pages through, and selects the appropriate map. "I must ask you to step away, Mitzy. And you too must keep your distance, Isadora. The subtlest shift in energies can interfere with this process."

"What process?" I eagerly lean in.

Silas wags his head with disappointment. "I'm going to have to ask you to step farther back, and apparently have a seat on the floor like a small preschool child, to prevent you from interfering."

I look at Grams and send her a quick telepathic message. *He's an angry little wizard.*

She giggles and pats a spot on the floor next to her.

The two of us sit down like kindergartners, or rather a kindergartner and her imaginary friend, on the first day of school.

Silas slips a small green glass bottle from inside his fascinating coat and pours a mound of reddish-brown granules into his palm. I want to ask him what it is, but I'm anxious to avoid further lectures.

We'd best keep quiet, Mitzy. He'll explain everything when he's ready.

Copy that. Thank heaven for telepathic communication.

Grams giggles.

Silas places his right hand over the left palm containing the tiny pile of granules, and he whispers a word that is for his ears only. He presses his hands together and rubs them in a circular motion.

To my confounded amazement, the granules flow out in a cloudy layer over the map. It's as though someone is holding a sheet of glass just a few inches above the map and then sprinkled this dust on top. The flakes are just floating on a horizontal plane in the air. It's pretty awesome.

Silas claps his hands briskly over the suspended cloud, and the granules contract and drop as though drawn by a strong magnet.

Once the little pile has formed on the map, Silas steps back.

"You may come closer."

I peer at the mysterious mound. "What is it?"

"They are iron filings."

I'm fascinated to discover that the granules have all collected over Fox Mountain.

I reach toward the map, for reasons I can't explain, and touch the red-brown slivers. Instantly, I receive a vision.

Rory, inside Brandy's house.

"He's in Brandy's house. Why would he go there?"

"Was it a vision or knowing?"

Before I can answer Silas, an additional image is delivered. "The bottle! He's looking for the potion bottle." I grab my phone and call the sheriff's station.

"Sheriff Harper, please. I know he's busy. This is about Rory Bombay. I know where he is."

That gets my call through. "Erick, he's in Brandy's house."

The line goes dead without so much as a "thank you."

Grams jumps to Erick's defense. "He'll thank you later, dear. You know how important it is for him to bring Rory in right away. I'm sure he just wanted to respond as quickly as possible, to avoid letting Mr. Bombay slip through his fingers."

I nod, but my feelings are a little hurt.

Glancing at Silas, I grin. "Now, are you going to

tell me why your spell—transmutation—worked when my pendulum wouldn't?"

He gently lowers himself into the over-stuffed, scalloped-back chair and nods thoughtfully. "Do you recall our discussion on the power of words?"

And we're off to the races with one of his tests. "Yes, I remember."

"And what knowledge did you take from that discussion?"

"That words have power. And something about native languages?"

"Perhaps you missed the deeper meaning."

"Obviously. What was the deeper meaning?"

"If words have power, it stands to reason that different words would carry alternate powers. Would you not agree?"

Throwing my hands up in the air, I respond with a hint of irritation. "I never know how to answer that question. Do I say, 'yes, I would not agree'? Do I say, 'no, I would not agree'? Either way I kinda feel like no matter what I say I'm not agreeing."

Silas harrumphs into his mustache. "A perfect example. You would first decide whether you are in agreement or not, and respond accordingly."

I roll my eyes. "Why didn't my pendulum work?"

"You made an imprecise request."

The hairs on the back of my neck tingle with anticipation. “And what request did you make?”

“I asked the iron filings to show me the man named Rory Bombay.”

I tilt my head. “I don’t think I see the difference?”

Silas steeples his fingers and bobs his chin before he replies, “You will.”

CHAPTER 20

THE NOW-FAMILIAR ROAD winding up Fox Mountain is deserted. When I pull into the parking lot, there are only two cars. I'll go out on a limb and guess that the news of Brandy's alleged involvement in the recent murder has put a dampener on ski-pass sales.

But I'm not here to ski. I'm here to do some ghost whispering.

Silas and Grams talked me into this strange mission, and the only reason I agreed was a flicker of hope that I would see Rory carted away in cuffs. The absence of flashing lights and sirens would indicate he's long gone. So, it looks like I'll be making good on my promise to Grams.

Since I have experience with a grand total of one ghost, I'm not entirely sure this mission will be successful. But my heart goes out to the woman who may be trapped on this side of the veil.

Walking directly to Brandy's cottage, I'm not surprised to find the door standing wide open. It's hard to say when Brandy would've been here last, but after Deputy Paulsen broke in to rescue me and Rory, no doubt, took advantage of the lack of security to retrieve the potion bottle, it looks like no one has been by to patch things up. I step into the home and scrape the busted door closed behind me.

I wander through the rooms, waiting to get some special psychic message, but nothing happens.

"Mrs. Schloss? Mrs. Schloss, I'm Mitzy Moon. We spoke the other night. I'm so sorry about Candy." The mood ring on my left hand grips my finger in an icy claw and the hairs on the back of my neck stand up as an angry spirit roars through the wall.

Terrified, I duck down behind the sofa. "Mrs. Schloss, I came to help. Please don't be mad."

An ominous voice bellows through the small cabin. "Get out!"

My teeth are chattering. I'm not sure if that's from fear or the fact that the temperature inside is now the same as the temperature outside. I slowly rise from my hiding spot. "Mrs. Schloss, I want to help you. I can help you move on."

The furious swirl of dark clouds in the room coalesces into the hunched woman I remember seeing several nights before.

Her spirit is broken and her face is etched with pain.

“Do you want to leave this place?”

“I can’t.”

“Why?”

“Someone has to take care of my baby girl. I always take care of my baby girl.”

I’m no psychologist, but something tells me more than one life ended the night Candy tangled with that moose on the moonlit slopes.

“It’s time for you to take care of yourself, Mrs. Schloss.”

“No. No. I have to set out the little reminders. And arrange the toys for her. She forgets. She forgets, you know.”

“Do you mean Brandy? Does Brandy forget?”

Her haunting laugh sends chills racing across my skin. “Oh no, dear. Brandy passed away. It’s my little Candy that I’m caring for. She likes her dollies arranged just so.”

Oh boy. This ghost is straight-up crazy town. Maybe Candy was her “favorite” and she couldn’t cope with losing her, so after she crossed over, she decided Brandy WAS Candy.

Although, technically, she didn’t cross over. She’s trapped in this house, tormenting herself and the *living* with her "never let go" obsession. I'm definitely not equipped for this. No easy solution comes to mind.

As I reach toward my mood ring to beg for assistance, my mother's face appears for a wavering moment. My heart aches with sadness. What I would say to her, if I had the chance?

Here goes nothing. "Candy wants you to rest. She's so grateful for everything you did for her, and she wants you to be free. She thought it would be okay to hang on to you, to keep you here, but she sees how tired you are and how much you need peace." I substitute Candy's name in place of the living twin, Brandy, since that's the name that triggers an emotional connection for Mrs. Schloss.

The ghost shimmers, and I recognize the sparkle of tears. "I am tired. But she needs me. Candy needs me."

"You'll always be in her heart. You've taken care of her for so long. Let me help you be at peace."

"I have to set up the toys. She always likes the way I set up her toys."

Based on my utter lack of real-life experience with ghosts, and relying solely on my extensive television expertise, I decide to take a page from *Supernatural*.

Somehow, Mrs. Schloss and her ghostly energy are tied to those toys. I can't very well start a fire inside the house. So I slowly, as non-threateningly as possible, move to the kitchen and search the drawers until I find a trash bag, some matches, and a lighter as a backup.

I run downstairs, scoop all the toys into the center of the blanket, fold it, and stuff everything into the garbage bag.

As I come back up the stairs an intimidating ghost blocks my way. "Where are you taking Candy's toys?"

"Candy wants me to take them to her." I'm not sure what the penalty is for lying to ghosts, but I'm extremely thankful this one doesn't have a telepathic connection to me.

I push through her ghostly essence and experience a bone-chilling cold.

All ghosts are not created equal.

Running into the bathroom, I grab a can of hairspray and rush outside. I drop the garbage bag in the snow, open it up, and spray everything with a thick layer of hairspray. I have to ditch the can to start lighting matches and dropping them on the pile. The hairspray catches quickly and I don't even need to use the lighter.

The ghost screams from inside the house.

This might've been a really bad idea. The flames begin to die as the layer of hairspray is consumed.

Picking up the can, I aim at the dying flames and spray.

Now, I'm not sure if you're completely familiar with how fire works, but let me break it down for you.

When you spray an accelerant into flames, you are basically holding a flamethrower.

I scream and throw the can into the fire.

Another stroke of genius.

Racing back into the house, I get behind the door just before the explosion. Now, that KA-BOOM is sure to attract the attention of the one or two employees still on site.

Time to wrap up this ghost business and vamoose.

"Mrs. Schloss? Mrs. Schloss?" There's no reply.

Closing my eyes, I reach out with my psychic feelers and hear a distant whimpering.

I follow the noise back down the stairs and into the basement.

There, beneath the steps, is the flickering ghost of Mrs. Schloss.

I reach toward her and pat her phantom back. "It's all right. You were a good mother. You can be with Candy now."

Her body begins to waver, like smoke in the wind.

And I'll never forget the look in her eyes or the

sound of her voice whispering, "Thank you," just before she vanishes.

Wiping my eyes, I hurry upstairs to avoid discovery.

When I peek out the front door, someone is standing over the smoldering ashes and shouting into their phone about a mysterious explosion.

I quietly make my way up the sidewalk, as many strides as I dare, before turning around. "Hey, everything okay? Are you all right? I thought I heard something."

The man turns, looks at me, and waves me off. "I'm on the phone with the cops."

I give him a "thumbs up" and race back to my Jeep.

Hopefully he'll forget he ever saw me, but I know one thing I'll never forget . . .

This day.

I'll never forget this day.

CHAPTER 21

Shockingly, I'm the last person in Pin Cherry Harbor to find out that Rory Bombay has been taken in for questioning. You would think with all the legwork I did on the case, I would've gotten a courtesy heads-up from Erick. No such luck.

However, I'm currently on my way to the sheriff's station to rectify this horrible oversight. I have an extensive list of my own questions I'd like to ask, not to mention using the ingenious alchemy that I think I've almost mastered. Silas has been forcing me to practice nonstop, but rather than be resentful I'm secretly thrilled with my progress.

If I can pull off this transmutation and slide away the veil of lies that Rory's been hiding behind, I might actually be able to expose the truth of Mr. Rory Bombay, if that is his real name.

Furious Monkeys must be on a break. The front desk at the station is empty. I march through the swinging wooden gate, fully prepared to put Deputy Paulsen in her place should she attempt to interfere, but the bullpen is also empty. No skin off my nose, I continue straight back to Erick's office—which is also empty.

Placing a hand on my hip, I stop and glance around the empty station. At that moment my mood ring sparks and sends a fiery blast up my left arm.

Time to pay attention. I close my eyes and let all of my senses open up to receive information. My heart rate immediately elevates and I feel adrenaline pulsing through my veins. It's not exactly fear, but there's definitely a heightened fight or flight response.

Glancing at my mood ring, I see the number "1." All right. I'm going to go with Interrogation Room One for the win.

Stepping out of Erick's office, I head straight for the door that I know too well. Somehow, in my haste to follow up on my psychic message, I trip over absolutely nothing and the full weight of my body smashes into the door as I turn the handle.

The door swings open with extreme force and blasts into something or someone.

Before I can apologize, Erick grabs a flying gun

—that was previously in Rory's hand—right out of midair, "Starsky-and-Hutch's" it across the interrogation table, grabs Rory by the arm, twists it behind his back, and slams his face down on the table.

"Holy *Bourne Identity*, Batman!"

Deputies Paulsen and Baird shove in behind me and I step into the corner to observe the strange events unfolding.

"Baird, get an extra set of cuffs." Erick is breathing heavily, but he's totally in charge.

I'm sorry to report, I'm a little turned on.

"10-4." Baird steps out.

"Paulsen, grab the manacles and the padlock. Looks like we're going to have to chain Mr. Bombay to the table if we want to complete this interrogation today."

I raise an eyebrow and take note of the extra twisting pressure Erick is applying to Rory's left arm.

"10-4." Paulsen shoots a look toward me that borders on admiration. I have no idea what I did, but I'll take it.

I smile.

She snarls and leaves the room.

While Erick and the two deputies are securing what I'm now assuming they're calling "their prisoner," I slip out and get a glass of water.

Oh, the water is not for me. I need a substance

to transmute with my truth symbols. I shakily hold the paper cup in one hand while I place my finger in the water and carefully trace the symbols Silas taught me. I definitely feel something shift in the liquid. I sincerely hope it's not my imagination.

By the time I return to Interrogation Room One, red-faced Rory Bombay is seated in the chair with his ankles locked together. A chain runs up through a second set of manacles on his wrists, loops through a metal ring on the interrogation table, and it is all secured with a menacingly large padlock.

"Hey, you look like you could use a drink. Here, let me help you."

I ignore Erick's frustrated exhale and focus on holding the energy of innocence. I put the cup to Rory's lips, and thankfully he gulps it down like a thirsty puppy.

Now, to test my work. The only decision left is: What do I most want to know? What is my burning question? Obviously, we'll get to the murder and Brandy, and everything associated with Fox Mountain. But what do I, Mitzy Moon, most want to know?

"Is your real name Rory Bombay?"

Rory's impudent green eyes look up at me, fill with horror, and his mouth forms a little "O" of surprise, right before the truth spills out. "No. My name is Frank Freeman."

I take a step back and smile with the deepest satisfaction I've felt since I quit my crappy barista job in Sedona. Crossing my arms, I glance at Erick and can't stop smiling.

Erick calls out to his deputy. "Paulsen, get the recorder in here."

A moment later she walks in, places the recording device on the interrogation table, and hits record. Erick steps up to the table, one hand firmly on his recently recovered gun, and announces, "This is Sheriff Erick Harper in Interrogation Room One with Rory Bombay a.k.a. Frank Freeman. Mr. Freeman, I'm going to inform you of your rights a second time, for the recording. You have the right to remain silent. Anything you say can and will be used against you in a court of law. You have the right to an attorney. If you cannot afford an attorney, one will be appointed for you. Do you understand these rights, as I've explained them to you?"

Again, Rory's eyes dart left and right in fear. "Yes." He swallows and shakes his head. He opens and closes his mouth as though he's trying to spit out a bad taste.

"Mr. Freeman, do we have your permission to

proceed with questioning and record this interview?"

"Yes," Rory hisses through clenched teeth.

"Mr. Freeman, what is your involvement with Brandy Hammer, formerly Brandy Schloss?"

"I . . . I needed . . . I needed a pawn. She's the reason Candy died. Cruel, entitled Brandy. She never should've inherited that resort. She stole Candy's life. I made something of myself, and I came back to make things right for Candy. Brandy was a desperate drunk, eager to believe in love. All I had to do was ply her with liquor and fan the flames."

I step closer to the table and look at him, with all of the psychic knowing I possess. "Did you pick up the love potion from Ania Karina Nowak?"

He clenches his jaw, but is unable to resist telling us the truth. "Yes," he growls.

"And did you add something to that potion?"

"Yes." He writhes against his chains.

Erick looks at me with an odd mixture of suspicion and admiration. "Mr. Freeman, in addition to the questions posed by Miss Moon, I would like you to tell me exactly what you put into the potion."

"Poison. Batrachotoxin."

"Where did you obtain this poison?"

"Columbia, South America. *Phyllobates terribilis*. Golden poison frog."

My eyes widen. If he just said "frog," and I'm

nearly positive he did, I'm never going to live this down with Robin Pyewacket Goodfellow.

Erick calmly continues his questioning. "And what was the purpose of this poison?"

"To frame Brandy Hammer for the murder of Oliver Kedrowski." Rory's mouth hangs open, and I see a tear leak from the corner of his left eye.

Erick looks at me and raises an eyebrow. "Mr. Freeman, why did you want Oliver Kedrowski dead?"

"He knew about my illegal land deal with the Natural Resources Department. He was going to ruin everything."

"Were you attempting to buy Fox Mountain?"

"Yes."

A couple of things fall into place and I jump in before Erick has a chance to continue. "Were you going to sell Fox Mountain to Harold Doherty?"

"Yes, along with the Legacy Land. The deal was worth millions. Make it stop, Mitzy. Make it stop."

Erick looks at me and shrugs his shoulders.

I smile and nod patronizingly at Rory. "I'm sorry I bumped into you as I entered the room, Frank. Are you all right?"

"You did something to me. You . . . you . . . you witch!"

Erick puts a hand on the table and leans toward

Rory. "I will ask you not to take that tone with a fine upstanding citizen like Miss Moon." He exhales and continues. "You confessed to the murder of Oliver Kedrowski, you confessed to an illegal land deal with the Natural Resources Department, and it seems you've also confessed to some potentially illegal real estate dealings with Harold Doherty."

A pained expression rips across Rory's visage. "Yes. Yes to all of it."

Erick lowers his voice. His menacing tone sends a shiver up my spine as he asks Rory the sixty-four-thousand-dollar question. "Why did you drag Mitzy into this?"

"I needed a witness. I needed someone like her with me when we found the body. She wouldn't sense anything, so she'd believe me." His gaze rips away from Erick and lands on me. "Make it stop!"

I'm beginning to worry that Rory may spill a bit too much truth. This would be that "double-edged sword" Silas warned be about. "Sheriff Harper, if you'll permit me, Mr. Freeman may need medical attention. He seems to be in some pain."

Erick nods. "One last thing, Mr. Freeman. Why were you holding me at gunpoint?"

"I just wanted to get out of here. I can't go to jail. I can't be Frank Freeman. I can't go back."

Since Silas didn't give me any instructions as to how to undo the transmutation, I have to assume it will continue until the energy burns out. I step toward Erick with every intention of leaving, but one more question pops into my mind. "Hey, Frank, how old are you?"

Rory fights this answer harder than any of the others, and I feel him struggling to find the energy to block the truth, but lucky for me he doesn't have that energy. "Forty-four."

I stare into his angry green eyes and search for any physical sign that he can possibly be that old. Whatever arcane knowledge he used to mask his age or slow his aging would fetch him a fortune in the beauty industry. Clearly it's not something he can bottle, or he would have. "Looks like I owe Silas an apology. Lose my number, Mr. Freeman."

"Ending interview with Mr. Freeman." Erick presses stop on the recording device.

As I place my hand on the doorknob, he makes one last comment. "Miss Moon, please give your full statement to Deputy Paulsen. And if you require any additional assistance, I'll be at Myrtle's Diner at 6:00 p.m."

"Copy that, Sheriff Harper."

Erick takes his eyes off the prisoner just long enough to give me a conspiratorial wink.

I nearly melt, but manage to get myself out of the room without tripping over anything.

I have almost no memory of giving my statement to Deputy Paulsen, which is great for me. I'm not sure how it turned out for her. All I can think of is how badly I need to get back to the bookshop, call Silas, and fill everyone in on the truth about Rory Bombay a.k.a. Frank Freeman.

CHAPTER 22

BURSTING with anticipation and a soupçon of pride, I race back to the Bell, Book & Candle to fill Grams in on my double success. Not only did I properly execute the truth symbols and facilitate a full confession from Frank "Rory Bombay" Freeman, but also I think I actually secured a date with Sheriff Too-Hot-To-Handle!

Triple success, if we're counting my ghost whispering.

Grams is beside herself with joy. And her flood of happy tears could certainly benefit from an afterlife handkerchief.

"You did a kind thing for that woman."

"I wonder if having her mother's ghost living in the house and moving things around is what drove Brandy to drink?"

"Could be, dear. I know how confused I felt when I first started getting my visions. If it hadn't been for Silas—who knows what I'd have done?"

"I can't believe she made up a whole other life, though. An imaginary husband and a kid? She actually made people call her 'Mrs. Hammer!'"

Grams shakes her head. "In her mind it was all real. Poor thing. Her family hid the truth about the accident being her fault to spare her feelings, but clearly she must've blamed herself for Candy's death."

"Rory, or rather Frank, sure did." Leaning against the solid wood of the bookcase, I sigh. "He spent his whole life putting together this revenge scheme. It's— It's insane."

"Tragedy tends to spiral, sweetie. Look at the effect your mother's death had."

Before those memories can shift into "replay," I stand and shake my whole body. "That's enough melancholy for one day, Grams. I have a DATE!"

She shifts gears instantly. "You're going to need an outfit!"

Before I can protest, she disapparates, and I know for certain she's in my couture-filled closet.

"Grams! Grams, it's a casual meal at Myrtle's. I can't go waltzing in there in one of your vintage Marchesa numbers." I pull the candle handle with my left hand. The bookcase slides open and I step into the apartment as Grams comes hurtling toward me.

"Heels? I'm thinking heels. He's a tall drink of water. You could easily get away with the five-inch Valentinos."

"Clearly you chose to ignore my request."

"What? I didn't hear any request, dear."

I don't need my extrasensory perception to recognize a massive ghost lie when I hear one.

"Mitzy! Judge not lest—"

"Grams!" I point meaningfully to my lips and shake my head.

"Oops." Her eyes twinkle with false apology and she vanishes back into the closet.

I repeat my list of reasons for a modest choice, and possibly make a tiny bit of headway.

"How about a pencil skirt—"

"How about you get to pick out a sweater and the jewelry. And I get to keep my dignity and my skinny jeans."

Grams crosses her arms over her ample bosom and exhales in frustration.

I roll my eyes. "You know what? You're almost as spoiled as Pyewacket."

And right on cue, "Ree-ow." Soft but condescending.

"I deserved that, Robin Pyewacket Goodfellow. You tried to tell me about the frog poison, and you were right about Rory from the very beginning. He deserved every hiss that you gave him."

"Reow." That one has a "better late than never" ring to it.

"Agreed. I will make an effort to take your warnings more seriously in the future. Let me make it up to you with a nice ear scratch, Mr. Cuddlekins."

Pyewacket struts over, lording his superior intellect over me, and I bend to thoroughly scratch behind both his ears.

His deep resonating purr thrums a healing chord in my heart.

"Enough spoiling. You need to start getting ready or you'll never have time to do your makeup properly."

A wave of mock-shock resets my features as I turn to Grams. "Hold on a minute. Are you telling *me* not to spoil the cat? Now there's a first, ladies and gentlemen."

"No time for scorecards. You get in there and put your face on."

I sit down at the marble-topped vanity and stare at my happy reflection. I get a flash of my mother's face and touch my lips, which are so like hers. Memories of sitting on the Formica counter in the bathroom of our studio apartment watching her "put on her face" wash over me. She would explain each step to me as though she were Xena, warrior princess, preparing for battle.

"This is called foundation and it covers up any weak spots or imperfections so I look ready to conquer the world."

Her voice always made me feel invincible.

"The blush gives me a little color so they can't tell I'm running on four hours' sleep."

She worked so hard to provide for me. I wonder if I was in day care as a toddler? Time erases so much.

"This cinnamon mocha lip tint gives me a confident smile, but keeps it professional."

Her smile made everything all right.

"A gentle application of smoky shadow gives my eyes depth and intelligence. Not that I'm not intelligent; this just confirms their suspicions."

Thanks for passing down the smarts, Mom.

"Always give the eyebrows a light nudge with a pencil, so you look like you mean business."

Then she would apply a little mascara to my lashes before she coated her own and finish by saying, "Dark lashes give you a finished look. Serious but mysterious." And she would kiss the tip of my nose, every single morning until—

I twist the mascara wand back into the tube and blink back the tears welling up in my eyes.

"I wish I could've known your mother, Mitzy." Grams gently strokes my hair.

I casually open the door to Myrtle's Diner at 5:59 p.m. My heart is filled with anticipation, but the rest of me is nervous that Erick might not show up.

Odell grins like a madman through the orders-up window and tilts his head toward the booth in the corner.

There, in all his civilian-clothed glory, is Erick "Yummy" Harper.

He stands and waves me over.

As I approach the table he extends his hand, but I shake my head.

I attempt to make a super-cool maneuver and sweep his hand aside and slide in for a hug, but my wonderful lack of coordination turns the entire event into a strange, slightly pokey "shug." Hashtag —Fail.

We both rush to avoid eye contact as we hastily slip into opposite sides of the booth.

"Thanks for the dinner invite." I smile and hope that I look sincere and not desperate.

"Thanks for your help with the interrogation this afternoon. I don't know what you put in Frank

Freeman's water, but that guy was singing like a canary."

I laugh too quickly and too loudly. If Erick had any idea what I actually put in Frank Freeman's water he'd probably run out screaming. "I think he wanted to get caught, you know. Once we confronted him with the evidence it seemed like it was a relief for him to confess."

Erick nods his head, but his eyes still hold a flicker of suspicion.

Time to change the subject. "By the way, you were pretty impressive yourself. With moves like that, you should be in the CIA or something."

Erick chuckles uncomfortably, but his eyes drift off to that faraway place where I can never follow.

"You okay?"

His gaze comes back to me, but his thoughts still seem focused in the past.

"What happened over there?"

His pupils dilate and his eyes target-lock on my face. "Maybe some other time."

"No time like the present. I'm sure it wasn't easy. What happened?"

Erick threads his fingers together, and unthreads them. He clenches his fists until his knuckles turn white and takes a deep breath. "It wasn't just one thing. It's not like in the movies where you make one wrong decision, lose a bunch of guys, and I'm the last man standing."

I nod with as much understanding as I can muster. I never served. How could I possibly know what it's like?

"It's just having to be on high alert every day, for so many days. The days turn into months. It takes a toll, you know?"

"Sounds exhausting."

"It's all the little things that add up. A lot of guys didn't come home. I don't feel bad that I did, I feel bad that they didn't. It doesn't get any easier. Each soldier that comes home in a box—it's just as hard as the one before."

"I can't imagine."

"I wrote their names in a little notebook I kept in my pocket. They say you're not really dead until you're forgotten. I wanted to make sure they were remembered."

I nod, but can't find any words.

"It was the worst when I first got back. I couldn't transition. So I didn't." He shifts his weight on the red vinyl bench seat and grips the edge of the table. "That first year, I kind of went off the rails. I let my hair grow wild, had an unkempt beard, and a raggedy mustache. I just hitchhiked around the country visiting every hometown of every soldier I lost. I didn't go see their families. I wasn't looking for sympathy and I didn't need to apologize, or anything." He pauses and nods. "It's a choice. You sign up, you know the drill. Some guys don't come home." He takes his spoon out of the napkin wrapper and stares at his reflection before buffing the silver surface. "But I visited every one of their hometowns, and I'd take a 'Go Army' sticker out of my backpack, write my soldier's name on it, and stick it on the back of each of the city limits' signs. I don't know why, or what it was supposed to mean. But it meant something to me at the time, and it meant that they weren't forgotten."

"I totally get it."

He looks across the table and clenches his jaw. "I know you get tired of me telling you to keep your nose out of things, Mitzy. But—I don't want to write any more names in the notebook."

His eyes glisten with emotion, and I have to dab my napkin at my own eyes to keep from bawling like a baby. "I appreciate it, Erick. Even though I don't always listen, I appreciate it." I'm about to reach across the table and pat his hand when Odell slides our meals onto the table.

He puts one hand on Erick's shoulder and gestures to me with his other thumb. "You done good, Sheriff."

Erick chuckles, and Odell's interference definitely breaks the tension and lightens the mood.

I slide my plate closer. "This looks great, Odell. Fries are perfect."

Erick and I dig into our meals and a comfortable silence settles on our table.

As I'm licking the last of my french-fry salt off my fingers, I catch Erick smiling at me with warm affection. I blush and look away.

Our thoughtful cook arrives moments later with two gorgeous slices of pin cherry pie and huge scoops of creamy vanilla ice cream slowly melting over each serving. "Enjoy."

"Mmmm." I reach for one of the plates. After a few bites of pie, a question pops into my head. "Hey, how did Rory manage to get your gun?"

Erick stops chewing and his shoulders sag. "I was trying to forget about that."

"Sorry, just curious."

He laughs as he wipes his mouth. "Aren't you always."

"Rude."

"It's a compliment. Your curiosity saved the day."

"But seriously, what happened?"

"I'm not entirely sure." Erick smooths the napkin in his lap before he continues. "One minute his hands were handcuffed behind him, and I was pacing beside the table trying to get him to crack.

And the next minute he's got my gun and he's threatening to shoot me if I don't let him go."

There's absolutely no way I'm going to explain to Erick that Rory possibly used some alchemical transmutation to escape from his handcuffs. I've got to say something though. "That is weird." I could've said something less lame than that. Before I can come up with a more intelligent commentary, the diner door scrapes open and Paulsen marches in.

"What is it, Paulsen?"

I turn to look over my shoulder and am surprised to see Paulsen grinning like the cat that swallowed—the goldfish, or some small creature.

"We've got something to show you and Kramer back at the station, Sheriff."

I look at Erick and shrug. "Kramer?"

He tries to hold in the laughter, but fails. "The deputies were in the observation room, between the interrogation rooms, working on a plan to take down Rory without getting me shot when you busted the door open and came sliding through. They started calling you Kramer after they witnessed your —entrance—"

"Kramer? From *Seinfeld*? Oh brother."

"We'll head over as soon as we finish our pie, Paulsen."

"See you in a couple minutes," she quips.

The diner door swishes closed and we hustle through our delicious desserts.

With a wave and an expression of our profuse gratitude, we head out of Myrtle's to the station.

Five or six deputies are gathered around the conference table, and someone's placed a large, flat-screen television at one end of the room.

Two chairs have been placed at the opposite end, and Erick and I are led to these places of honor.

"I hope none of you are on overtime. You don't get paid for practical jokes around here." Erick's attempt at sounding gruff is met with a round of laughter.

"Sit tight, Sheriff. It's worth every penny." Paulsen turns off the lights, while one of the other deputies hits play.

I immediately recognize the closed-circuit feed from Interrogation Room One, and I see Rory, handcuffed, seated in a chair, as Erick indeed paces beside the table.

There's no audio, but I see Rory's lips moving.

For some reason, even though I'm watching a video and it's not happening live, I can sense the exact moment Rory slips free of his handcuffs. Maybe it's a new twist on my abilities, but the pride and malice is palpable. I watch him bide his time, waiting for Erick to pace past him and turn his back.

Like a cobra, Rory strikes. He draws the gun and waves of threatening energy turn my stomach.

Erick backs against the wall and lifts his hands.

"Thanks, guys. This is definitely a moment I want to relive." Erick shakes his head.

Deputy Baird eagerly pipes up, "Hang on, Sheriff. It gets better."

Rory backs toward the door and waves the gun menacingly.

A moment later the door flies open, smacking Rory in the back and knocking the gun into the air. And that is indeed when things get better.

With the speed and precision of a mongoose, Erick snatches the gun out of midair, slides across the table, and performs one of the most impressive takedowns ever caught on film!

The six deputies in the room jump to their feet with a standing ovation for the sheriff.

Erick blushes and shakes his head. "Just a lucky break, guys. Sit down, sit down."

Paulsen adds her two cents. "Don't worry, Sheriff. Kramer over there gets at least half the credit."

Guffaws and a brief chant of "Kramer! Kramer! Kramer!" fills the room and I get my chance to redden with embarrassment.

Deputy Baird gives me a little wink before she

says, "That's all the entertainment we've got, Sheriff. We'll let you two get back to your date."

An awkward silence settles on the room, and Erick stands abruptly. "Why don't I walk you back to the bookshop, Moon."

My soaring heart sinks a little when I hear him say my last name. Seems like a lifetime ago when we sat in the diner and shared a tender moment and he called me Mitzy. Oh well, *c'est la vie.*

We walk out of the sheriff's station in silence, but about halfway down the block Erick slips his hand in mine.

It takes every ounce of self-control, that I don't possess, for me not to jump up and down and squeal like a high-school girl. I never knew holding hands could be such a thrill.

We reach the front door of the bookshop too soon, and I fumble to extract my beautiful, triangle-barreled brass key from the chain around my neck.

"Thanks for dinner, Erick."

"Thanks for saving my life, Moon."

"I figure I owed you one."

He chuckles. "Let's see what we can do about keeping you on the straight and narrow."

I leave the key in the lock and turn toward him, hand on hip. "I'd hate to see you set yourself up for disappointment, Erick."

His eyes soften and he steps near. "You never disappoint me."

My tummy flips and my skin tingles as his hand brushes my cheek. Oh boy! This is it. It's happening. In the movies, face touching always precedes the big kiss. I let my eyelids flutter—

RING! RING! RING!

Erick tenses up, pulls away, and reaches in his pocket to silence his phone. "Sorry, I thought I had that turned off." His cheeks flush handsomely, and, to his credit, he tries again.

This time his hand slides around my waist and I lean into him—

"Sheriff! Sheriff Harper! He's escaped!" Deputy Baird is standing in the middle of the sidewalk waving her arms like an inflatable airdancer.

Before he has a chance to ask, I blurt out the knowledge that hits me like a ton of rotten eggs. "It's Rory. He escaped."

Erick is all business now. "When?"

"The transport vehicle went off the road."

"Ellis and Lundberg?"

"Lundberg has a broken arm and Ellis has a concussion. Doc says they'll both be fine."

He exhales and nods. Relief floods though him. "And the prisoner?"

"Vanished. Manacles left in the back seat. Some blood on the broken window, but not enough."

He turns toward me and opens his mouth.

I put up a hand. "No explanation needed. And I don't mean to be a pessimist, but Rory has money and connections. He'll be out of the country before you even issue the BOLO."

"You're probably right, but I gotta do it anyway. Raincheck?"

I grin mischievously. "For what?"

"For our date."

"Your terms are agreeable."

"G'night, Mitzy."

"Night, Sheriff."

He jogs toward the station, shaking his head and laughing under his breath.

Look at me! I had a date.

I almost had a kiss.

And now I have a tantalizing raincheck.

Will wonders never cease!

End of Book 5

A NOTE FROM TRIXIE

Another case solved! I'll keep writing them if you keep reading . . .

The best part of "living" in Pin Cherry Harbor continues to be feedback from my early readers. Thank you to my alpha readers/cheerleaders Angel and Michael. HUGE thanks to my fantastic beta readers who continue to give me extremely useful and honest feedback: Veronica McIntyre, Renee Arthur, and Nadine Peterse-Vrijhof. And big "small town" hugs to the world's best ARC Team – Trixie's Mystery ARC Detectives!

Much appreciation to my steadfast editor Philip Newey! Some authors dread edits, but it is always a pleasure to work with Philip, and I look forward to many more. Any errors are my own.

I certainly owe a heaping helping of gratitude to

the real-life Ania, who studied my text and found the perfect Polish word for Silas to use in his big scene! *Dziękuję Ci.* (*In case I messed up, that's supposed to be "Thank you" in Polish!*)

Now I'm writing book seven in the Mitzy Moon Mysteries series, and I think I may just live in Pin Cherry Harbor forever. Mitzy, Grams, and Pyewacket got into plenty of trouble in book one, *Fries and Alibis*. But I'd have to say that book three, *Wings and Broken Things*, is when most readers say the series becomes unputdownable.

I hope you'll continue to hang out with us.

Trixie Silvertale (March 2020)

BARS AND BOXCARS

Mitzy Moon Mysteries 6

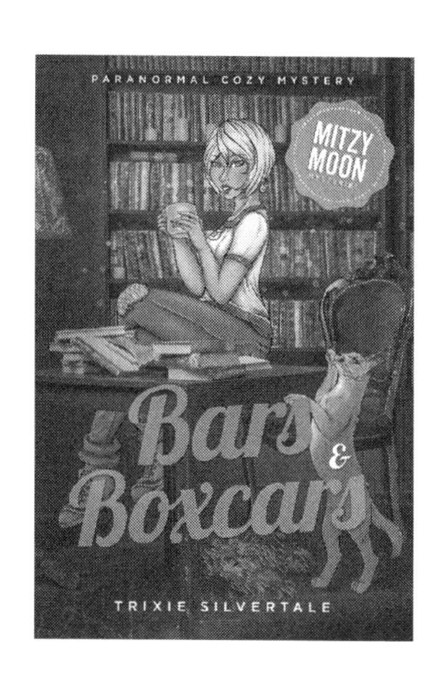

A robbery on the rails. A gang in hiding. Can this psychic sleuth blow the whistle on a dangerous crew?

Mitzy Moon struggles to put snooping on the back burner and help launch the Duncan Restorative Justice Foundation. But her good-girl routine leaves the station after a deputy crashes the Grand Opening with a search warrant. And she's full-steam ahead on the case when she discovers her father's railroad is the target for a heist.

Never one to play it safe, Mitzy blatantly ignores the warnings of her entitled feline and risks everything. She even cons her interfering Ghost-ma into helping her with an alarming undercover plan. And now she promises just a few more shifts at the seedy roadhouse and she'll have the crooks stopped in their tracks.

Can Mitzy pull off the double cross of a lifetime, or will more than her investigation be derailed?

Bars and Boxcars is the sixth book in the hilarious paranormal cozy mystery series, Mitzy Moon Mysteries. If you like snarky heroines, supernatural intrigue, and a dash of romance, then you'll love Trixie Silvertale's twisty whodunits.

Buy *Bars and Boxcars* to climb aboard a mystery today!

Scan this QR Code with the camera on your phone. You'll be taken right to the Mitzy Moon Mysteries series page. You can easily grab any mysteries you've missed!

SPECIAL INVITATION . . .

Come visit Pin Cherry Harbor!

Get access to the Exclusive Mitzy Moon Mysteries character quiz – free!

Find out which character you are in Pin Cherry Harbor and see if you have what it takes to be part of Mitzy's gang.

This quiz is only available to members of the Paranormal Cozy Club, Trixie Silvertale's reader group.

Click the link below to join the club and get access to the quiz:

Join Trixie's Club
http://trixiesilvertale.com/paranormal-cozy-club/

Once you're in the Club, you'll also be the first to receive updates from Pin Cherry Harbor and access to giveaways, new release announcements, behind-the-scenes secrets, and much more!

Scan this QR Code with the camera on your phone. You'll be taken right to the page to join the Club!

THANK YOU!

Trying out a new book is always a risk and I'm thankful that you rolled the dice with Mitzy Moon. If you loved the book, the sweetest thing you can do (*even sweeter than pin cherry pie à la mode*) is to leave a review so that other readers will take a chance on Mitzy and the gang.

Don't feel you have to write a book report. A brief comment like, "Can't wait to read the next book in this series!" will help potential readers make their choice.

Leave a quick review HERE
https://readerlinks.com/l/962809

★★★★★

Thank you kindly, and I'll see you in Pin Cherry Harbor!

ALSO BY TRIXIE SILVERTALE

MITZY MOON MYSTERIES

Fries and Alibis: Paranormal Cozy Mystery

Tattoos and Clues: Paranormal Cozy Mystery

Wings and Broken Things: Paranormal Cozy Mystery

Sparks and Landmarks: Paranormal Cozy Mystery

Charms and Firearms: Paranormal Cozy Mystery

Bars and Boxcars: Paranormal Cozy Mystery

Swords and Fallen Lords: Paranormal Cozy Mystery

Wakes and High Stakes: Paranormal Cozy Mystery

Tracks and Flashbacks: Paranormal Cozy Mystery

Lies and Pumpkin Pies: Paranormal Cozy Mystery

Hopes and Slippery Slopes: Paranormal Cozy Mystery

Hearts and Dark Arts: Paranormal Cozy Mystery

Dames and Deadly Games: Paranormal Cozy Mystery

Castaways and Longer Days: Paranormal Cozy Mystery

Schemes and Bad Dreams: Paranormal Cozy Mystery

Carols and Yule Perils: Paranormal Cozy Mystery

Dangers and Empty Mangers: Paranormal Cozy Mystery

Heists and Poltergeists: Paranormal Cozy Mystery

Blades and Bridesmaids: Paranormal Cozy Mystery

Scones and Tombstones: Paranormal Cozy Mystery

Vandals and Yule Scandals: Paranormal Cozy Mystery

More to come!

MAGICAL RENAISSANCE FAIRE MYSTERIES

Explore the world of Coriander the Conjurer. A fortune-telling fairy with a heart of gold!

Book 1: ***All Swell That Ends Spell*** – A dubious festival. A fatal swim. Can this fortune-telling fairy herald the true killer?

Book 2: ***Fairy Wives of Windsor*** – A jolly Faire. A shocking murder. Can this furtive fairy outsmart the killer?

MYSTERIES OF MOONLIGHT MANOR

Join Sydney Coleman and her unruly ghosts, as they solve mysteries in a truly haunted mansion!

Book 1: ***Moonlight and Mischief*** – She's desperate for a fresh start, but is a mansion on sale too good to be true?

Book 2: ***Moonlight and Magic*** – A haunted Halloween tour seem like the perfect plan, until there's murder...

Book 3: ***Moonlight and Mayhem*** – An unwelcome visitor. A surprising past. Will her fire sale end in smoke?

ABOUT THE AUTHOR

USA TODAY Bestselling author Trixie Silvertale grew up reading an endless supply of Lilian Jackson Braun, Hardy Boys, and Nancy Drew novels. She loves the amateur sleuths in cozy mysteries and obsesses about all things paranormal. Those two passions unite in her Mitzy Moon Mysteries, and she's thrilled to write them and share them with you.

When she's not consumed by writing, she bakes to fuel her creative engine and pulls weeds in her herb garden to clear her head (*and sometimes she pulls out her hair, but mostly weeds*).

Greetings are welcome:
trixie@trixiesilvertale.com

Made in the USA
Las Vegas, NV
25 January 2023

66243941R00166